Praise for N

Song of the Crocodile

'Throughout the novel, there are stunning moments of perfect fluidity and permeability, where Simpson's deep engagement with the ancestries and cosmology of her people comes through. Simpson's writing attains a rare quality of grace, the prose lyrical and grounded at the same time … skilfully weaving the profound into the everyday' *Saturday Paper*

'Exquisite … Simpson explores the enduring legacy of violence and racism, in a narrative enriched by beautiful descriptions of the landscape' *Sydney Morning Herald*

'Lyrical and evocative' *Sunday Age*

'This beautiful debut novel drips with evocative descriptions of the land' *The Australian Women's Weekly*

'A beautiful work' *New Idea*

'A lightning debut' Kill Your Darlings

'A beautifully written and moving novel' Good Reading

Also by Nardi Simpson

Song of the Crocodile

the belburd

nardi simpson

hachette
AUSTRALIA

hachette
AUSTRALIA

Published in Australia and New Zealand in 2024
by Hachette Australia
(an imprint of Hachette Australia Pty Limited)
Gadigal Country, Level 17, 207 Kent Street, Sydney, NSW 2000
www.hachette.com.au

Hachette Australia acknowledges and pays our respects to the past and present Traditional Owners and Custodians of Country throughout Australia and recognises the continuation of cultural, spiritual and educational practices of Aboriginal and Torres Strait Islander peoples. Our head office is located on the lands of the Gadigal people of the Eora Nation.

Copyright © Nardi Simpson 2024

A catalogue record for this
work is available from the
National Library of Australia

ISBN: 978 0 7336 4796 3 (paperback)

Cover design by Christabella Designs
Cover illustrations courtesy of Getty Images; Shutterstock
Typeset in Bembo Std by Kirby Jones
Printed and bound in Australia by McPherson's Printing Group

The paper this book is printed on is certified against the Forest Stewardship Council® Standards. McPherson's Printing Group holds FSC® chain of custody certification SA-COC-005379. FSC® promotes environmentally responsible, socially beneficial and economically viable management of the world's forests.

For ngaannguwaa-bala ngurrambaa

'Some of the greatest poetry is revealing to the reader the beauty in something that was so simple you had taken it for granted.'

Neil deGrasse Tyson

Part One

the mound

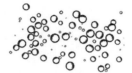

1.

Blak Love

Ginny wanted to get there as early as she could. Not too early to risk looking like a tragic, but early enough to scope out the place, see how the open mic worked. She parked in the alley. The spot was a no-standing zone. She didn't care. She grabbed her bag, locked the car, and began walking through the pungent, bin-clogged backstreet that led to the university campus. Cutting through would shave a few minutes off the walk and help her avoid the greasy side streets that slid into creepiness as soon as the sun began to fall. Then it would be a scurry through an art spattered tunnellish laneway to the park, across which the uni's bookshop-come-bar-come-cafe venue stood.

Ginny, expert at shortcuts, quickly made it to the poster-lathered underpass. The soles of her scruffy white Cons squeaked against the concrete, the echo shooting down the tunnel walls. These were lathered in years of glue and spray-painted slogans. It was so uni. Just like all the student types she watched scurry around. Seemingly chaotically carefree but actually cultivated and self-aware. She read what she could of the posters as she passed. Marches and gigs and calls to action. Strikes and shows and revues and recitals. Pink and silver and fluoro yellow streaks popped from the shadowy, lettery word soup.

A moment before the tunnel ended, a bleached patch of white caught her eye. It was only a scrap of paper, a twinkle in the smudge-stained streak. But its clarity found its way to her from beneath the faded tags and congealed paste.

Ginny stopped in front of the paper. *Contribute work to Smart Cookie Press, an independent, student-run printing and publishing collective.*

In the sea of expansive, printed bill posters, the modest A4 beamed at her. *Stories, prose, music and poetry all accepted.* A naive, hand-drawn illustration, obviously Smart Cookie's logo, portrayed a squat, sprawling tree with purple leaves. Ginny knew the very one. It was in the Main Quad, hemmed by sandstone walkways and squares of manicured grass. She looked at the flickers of paper that hung from the bottom of the page. Strips of *Smart Cookie Press* with a mobile number curled like fake eyelashes. She stared. Then blinked. The fluoro light bounced off the numbers. She leaned closer and raised her hand, running her fingertips over the paper's curl. A wash of voices filled the tunnel. Ginny retreated then continued through the tunnel and across the park.

At the shop's entrance she was surprised to hear the tinkle of coffee cups. A small grouping of tables seated long-haired girls chatting and sipping. Chai, most probably, this time of evening. She never understood the drink herself. But over a billion Indians couldn't all be wrong. And she figured it would probably come into its own around about now, in these parts, at this kind of do. Chicks round here were definitely the types who had rules about caffeine intake and bloating and rest and hydration, blah, blah, blah. Sidling past the clinking, she made her way to a covered courtyard. Ginny paused in the doorway, taking it in. She could see a brick wall running the yard's entire length. A stage was squashed, haphazard, into its middle. Set on its tiny platform was a rounded table with a stack of colour-coded books. A salvaged school chair nestled near the table. This dressing almost took up the entirety of the stage. A microphone and stand teetered at the rise's edge. Ginny noticed most of the tables and chairs that would presumably hold an audience were oriented to face the opposite direction of the stage. She followed their alignment to the far end of the courtyard and an already humming bar. Fairy lights draped from wooden beams and plastic corrugated roofing. Blended families of ferns clustered in corners. The entire space was filled with the orange and cinnamon scent of warming mulled wine.

'Excuse me,' said a slender man inching past.

Ginny shuffled against the wall, her heart pounding a bit. Sensing she might pike she blurted, 'Do you know where I put my name down?'

As he moved closer to her, he stepped on the absolute end of her first two toes.

'Sorry.' He winced. 'For … ?' he continued, his eyebrows arching as he shot a look up then down her frame.

Ginny straightened, raising her chest to the challenge. 'The open mic. I'm not just a pretty face.'

'The what?' he bent towards her, cocking an incredibly long lobe.

'The poetry reading,' she answered, her voice cresting over the waves of raucous conversation. He was so close, Ginny observed the transition of ear hair into sideburn. She shuffled backwards.

'Oh, that's right, it's poetry night,' the man replied, straightening. 'Ah …' He scanned the heads of the growing crowd. 'That guy,' he said, gesturing with his glass. 'In the Himalayan yak vest.' His wine glass full of red liquid and ice cubes tinkled towards the bar.

The guy in question was in the middle of a puddle of people. He lounged against the bar, his shoulder-length hair glinting in the fairy lights as he spoke.

Ginny clocked the vest and pressed her lips together, holding tight to the chuckle trying hard to escape. The fluffy fabric's lavender, indigo and blush patches accentuated his bare, tanned arms. High-waisted jeans with short hems framed sockless, dress-shoed feet. All eyes were on him. And Ginny could see, from the pulled-back shoulders and promoted jawline, that he knew it.

'Thanks,' she said, sucking in a deep breath and snaking through the mismatched tables and bench chairs towards him.

The group, mostly women, made a tight circle around the guy, so she loitered for a bit.

'And Fabs, will you read tonight?' a woman said, draping herself on his forearm.

'Ooh yes, Fabs, you must.'

'I wasn't intending to,' he replied, shaking a coil of mousy-blond strands from his cheek, 'although I do have the germ of an idea that's really been gnawing ...'

'You have to do it!'

'Yes, Fabian, it will be wonderful. But you already know that!'

He bowed his head then and sipped, ceremoniously, at his drink.

Ginny pushed into the circle. 'Hi!' she announced. 'Is this where I put my name down?'

The group turned. She felt them scan her. She didn't care, she'd already done it to them. Sussed every one of them. And they were all a version of the same theme. Privileged playing at boho. Definitely students, arts faculty most likely. Cotton skirts and flowing rayon shuffled, giving her space. *Tree of Life mannequins come to life*, she thought. Ginny laugh-snorted, the waft of sandalwood rising from the circle, enhancing the joke.

Fabs stepped forward, eyes brightening as he took her in. 'Enchanté,' he said, taking Ginny's hand and bringing it to his lips. They were yucko warm.

Ginny tugged her hand free and wiped it on the back of her jeans. A handful of women peeled away from the group and moved further down the bar.

'Reading for the first time?' Fabs continued, sweeping over Ginny's collarbones and neck before staring directly into her eyes.

Ginny nodded. She held his gaze.

'I see you've come by yourself. Creative. Brave.' He nodded. 'You are most definitely in the right place.'

'So, how's it work?'

Fabs reached round to the bar and produced a clipboard. Stuck to it was a blank sheet of white paper. 'Write down your name and the title of your work, and I'll call you up at some stage to perform. Or read. We don't expect all our first timers to have memorised their work. Our audience is very supportive of all our virgins.' He laughed.

Ginny stared. *Creep*, she thought.

Fabs smiled, vacant and oblivious, then fumbled in his back pocket and pulled out a biro. He thrust both it and the clipboard into Ginny's hand.

She took them, scrunching her nose at the transferred warmth lingering on the pen.

'I like to do a few pieces to start with. To warm up the crowd. Get them ready to … engage.' His smile spread too wide – it was fake as. 'Then, if there are any experienced poets, I usually call on them. Most times I have friends keen to read or try out ideas. We're a close-knit group, us poets. Maybe you could join our writing group,' he said. Before she could reply, he continued, 'Anyway, then I'll curate a flow with the names I have. I position new poets between artists whose work I know. That way it doesn't feel like a competition.' He stopped. 'How's that sound, Miss …'

Ginny shuffled and looked down at the board. Too late to back out now. 'Dilboong.'

'Dil-bung,' he copied, incorrectly. 'Dil-bung,' he repeated. 'Are you … a sista by any chance?'

'You mean Indigenous?' she said, cautiously.

'Yes, forgive me if I'm using incorrect terminology. Are you Indigenous?'

'Yes.'

Fab's body straightened. His face lit up.

'Miss Dil-bung. Would you do us the honour of welcoming us to country tonight? It would be deadly if we could ground the night in deep respect.'

'I don't—'

'It would be such a magnificent way to start the evening! And might even help shift some of the early nerves.' He shrugged, moving close to her. 'We've all been to events where the welcome is mere formality. Boring. Gammon,' he added with a laugh. 'Miss Dil-bung, a welcome by you would infuse the night with poetic propriety.' He paused, filling his chest with air, fingertips spread upon his expanded, faux-Tibetan chest.

'Poetic propriety?'

'Yes, it will make everything sing.'

Ginny laughed hard. She felt the belly above her jeans wobble. When she looked back at Fabs she realised he was serious.

'I'm … not—'

'Not … ?' He pouted, shaking his lips towards the unfinished sentence.

'I'm …' She flung her arm and wrist out in a flick she hoped would finish the sentence on her behalf.

'But you are Indigenous?'

'Yeah,' she said, the word bouncing in refrain.

'Indigenous to Australia?' he questioned, leaning on the end of the sentence.

'So called,' she replied.

'Hang on,' he said, tugging at the bottom of his vest. 'You are Aboriginal, correct?'

'Yeah, I'm Blak,' Ginny declared.

'I'm sorry,' Fabs said, bending towards her as he waved to a group sauntering past, 'I'm not quite catching your drift then.'

'I won't welcome anyone.'

Fabs frowned.

'Maybe you're not welcome—'

'Ohh,' Fabs exclaimed. 'I am so incredibly sorry, Miss Dilboone,' he mangled. Ginny sighed. 'I should know better. I beg your pardon. Acknowledgement. I mean to ask for the blessing of an acknowledgement.'

Ginny stood. Silent and still.

'Would you perform an acknowledgement for us tonight? Before we begin?' he added quickly. 'We would be so honoured,' he said, stooping into a slight bow while motioning to the bartender for a refill.

Ginny chose her words carefully. 'It's not – appropriate,' she said. Fabs' pretend listening, fake-smile-smirk-bow made her add, 'when there's so much grog around.'

'Oh.' He smarted, accepting his fresh tumbler of mulled wine. 'Of course.' He took a sip. 'In that case, you better register.'

'You mean this?' Ginny raised the clipboard, its bleached, blank page reflecting warm yellow light.

'New readers have to register if they want to be considered for a spot on the night. Of course, experienced, regular artists, don't need to. The quality of their work is known.'

He sniffed as she wrote her name on the page. When she was done Fabs slid both the clipboard and pen from Ginny's grasp. He tossed them onto the bar. The biro whirred in a circle a few times then fell onto the floor. 'Hopefully we'll have time to hear your work, Jenny.' Fabs then turned from her and dissolved into a group bulging at the bar.

By the time Fabs finally called her name, most of the crowd were sloshed. They huddled in small groups, chatting or scrolling or typing into their phones. She stepped onto the stage and placed her lips near the microphone. She breathed, deep and long. A warmth came into her centre. It reminded her that all this had already happened. She had already read it and left and had lived her life. She had also never met Nathan yet. Was minding her own business and snuggling up to her body pillow every night. Holding her notebook but closing her eyes, she drenched herself in Dreaming, and began.

Blak Love

Our particular form of Blak love

Began on DM. Pictorial mostly.

Fruits, flames, pounding hearts

Bitten lip emojis

Had me hungry

Blak-love-laced cupcakes

Crusts dark, middles creaming

Nibbled and oozing

Our particular version of Blak love

Was strewn across corners of

Sterile hotel rooms

Until the island where

Rising mountain and swelling river

Made children of us

Your toes wriggled in freshly washed socks

My head cradled in your lap, dream-wishing

Our specific way of Blak lovin

Was served on platters of salt-sweetness

Olive and oyster

Freshly caught prawns

Breakfast, juice, beer

Lust garnished entrees

of mis-served attention

Gorging ourselves on opportunist greed

Our particular form of Blak love

Probably wasn't love at all

It was short, like me.

And sweet, like you.

Your flavour lingers

Today we are Blak

And strangers.

Opening her eyes, she added in a quiet but certain voice, 'Ginny Dilboong'.

2.

It was Eel Mother who told me I began as a bubble from a whale. 'Great Whale himself,' she said, 'sent you to me. And you have been the greatest gift I think I've ever received.'

Farts are funny, so I laughed. My bubble wobble-jiggled picturing Great Whale's fart.

She saw my chuckle in the ripples that pushed from my sac. An irritated flash shot up her floppy sides. The colour glinted into her eyes. She took a swipe at me with her tail.

'Not that end,' she said. 'Great Whale doesn't pop off like everyone else.'

'I was a burp?' I blurted. 'Gross.'

There was a rumbling near where my gut button and bum cheeks might grow. It could have been another laugh. I held on to this one though, sucking all my squish innards as tight as I could. The effort made me feel wonky. I started seeing things.

Somewhere around where my eyes were going to form, my idea space or head spirit or something, a whale swam into view. Singing and swishing, a line of burps rose from the whale's spout. Kind of like drool. But the wrong way up. Imaginary Great Whale winked his beady eye then squeezed a tiny toot out from under his meaty tail.

I wobble-roared. That laugh had a lot of power in it. I guess most inside things do. Eel Mother watched my cackle twist itself into a rising whirlpool. It fizzed all the way up to the surface, into the above.

She swiped at me again. This time I went somersaulting into the current that crouched at the edge of her lair. It pulled me towards the sea floor. I watched flashes of apricot and green run up and down Eel Mother's saggy sides. She sure was floppy. And colourful. I loved her a lot.

'Not so clever now, are you, little Sprite?' she said. 'It's pretty dark down there,' she went on, teasing. 'Who knows what terrible kinds of crawly things live on the sea floor? I'd watch out if I were you.'

I wasn't frightened, twisting and falling into the depths. I was safe inside my sac. Plus, I could still see Eel Mother, her head bobbing over the sandstone overhang. All teeth and flashes of coloured body light. It was fun spinning and churning and wobbling in the warm, salt flow. If they had existed, I would have chucked out my arms. I loved the water. But I also wanted to fly.

She left me to bobble on the bottom for a while. I wanted to wave at a silly looking prawn, cause I thought he waved first, but it turned out he just had a billion arms that moved all the time.

From the bottom of the harbour I watched Eel Mother's body deflate before expanding and getting full again. She sucked me back with a huge inhale – drawing me back in a rip, directly towards her jaggedy teeth. Rocketing upwards, I watched her crank open her jaws. After I gushed in, she shut down tight, trapping me inside. The force of the slipstream whacked me into the roof of her mouth.

'Geeze,' I said. 'Not so hard!' I told her. 'You're not half as floppy on the inside, you know.'

She clicked me around. I bounced off her tongue a few times. When I stopped spinning, she spat me out on the ledge right under her cheek crevice. Amber pooled in its sag. The colour seeped into her neck lines, highlighting the wrinkles that dragged her bulk onto the cave floor.

Eel Mother peered down at me. She was trying to look serious. Her happyish colours didn't help. Also, a sea louse squirmed from a roll of fat beneath her chin.

I shifted, hoping not to laugh and make another spiralling mirth spout again.

Her eyes widened. She leered harder.

I butted in, mostly to stop myself from laughing again. 'Sorry, Eel Mother,' I sang.

'For?'

'Joking around. And rousing at you. And probably not really listening to anything you say.'

Her eye sockets softened. 'You're a cheeky one,' she said. 'And,' she paused, maybe deciding if her next words were true, 'I shouldn't, but I love you for it.' Her chin fluttered in the current.

The water around me softened. Supposing it was an Eel Mother hug I relaxed. 'Is Great Whale your boyfriend?'

She lowered her head on a mound of body fat. Fluorescent green grasses tickled edges of smooth stones.

'He is,' she said slowly, 'my dearest and oldest friend. I've known him since this cove was a trickle.'

I knew Eel Mother was old. Ancient, most probably. Her body was long and fat and draggy. She took up most of my world. Until then, I never thought that she might have wanted more.

'Were you ever a bubble, a soul egg, like me?' I asked.

'No,' she replied. Her all-over grey was now twinkling with sad specks of gold. 'I came straight from a mother. And had brothers and sisters galore.' Through a stretchy smile, she took in a gulp. Then fanned it out her gills. The jets creased the water so that thousands of wiggly strips burst out and jiggled upstream. Their flapping looked funny. For some reason I felt sad watching her family dissolve into the openness.

'When will I get my family?' I asked her. Brothers and sisters would probably be fun. And a father would be good to have too – although I didn't know much about them. All I really hoped for, more than anything in my bubbly, watery life, was a mother. In the above. Waiting just for me.

Eel Mother scooped me up and slithered us into the dark of her cave. Beneath me, her head and body turned night-time blue. She was so dark she was shining! Her twinkly gold flecks got happier and brighter. Her body's flickering reflection bounced off the cave walls and shone a pathway to the back of her lair. Her movement and shine made strange shapes rise up the walls. Eel Mother was good at that sort of thing. She always showed me stuff I didn't know was there.

The mound emerged. Gazillions of fidgeting, birth spirit balls were stacked on top of each other. Towering into a fine point. The soul eggs were mostly pearl coloured. I loved that rows of birth spirit heads were cradles for the bums of those above. For them and for me, heads and bums weren't actual things yet. If they were, I would be gazing into seas of them, all squished into each other. Then

I would have laughed a burst that could have rocketed me to the other side of the sea.

'I think a visit is in order, Sprite,' Eel Mother said.

'But I already know about the mound,' I told her as she moved me onto the tip of her beak. 'I live at its base, next to you.'

Eel Mother surged upwards. I lurched. It was hard to hold on to things as an egg bubble.

'Relax, little Sprite. You won't fall,' she told me, waves of excitement tensing and releasing along her body.

Swimming upwards, we climbed. We rose for what seemed like an age, zooming past the swaying bubbles. I jumped and shouted inside my casing. I'd spoken to heaps of birth spirits before, but never ones so young and high up. They hadn't slipped far enough towards the cave floor for me to know them yet. They were long lifetimes away from Eel Mother taking them to go into a mum.

From what I could tell zooming past, the spirits were pleased to see me. Swirls of rose and lilac flushed through them as we went. Reaching the top, Eel Mother slowed. We bobbled above the humongous pile. Her body was straight. Still saggy, but strong. Even though we could barely make out the cave floor, lots of leftover Eel Mother still coiled around the mound's base. I watched her tail swish pulses of water over the bottom of the pile. The lower birth spirits squealed as they twirled in the freshness, aerating in place. I edged myself away from her wrinkle and peered down.

'I didn't know it was this big.'

She smiled, bobbing.

'Won't it take ages for them to get where they need to be?' She was so silent and her breathing so slow I suddenly wasn't sure she was still awake. So I shouted, 'When do I get to be born, Eel Mother?'

Her body tightened. Her smile slipped a little and went weird, melting into an empty stretch of lips.

'Take your time,' she told me. Then she tossed her head backwards. The movement flung me from her, plopping me onto the highest handful of spirits. Swallowed by their slippery circles, and feeling the retreating waft of Eel Mother's descent, I trickled through the massed funnel, gliding between the smoothness. Falling.

3.

'It's Sprite, come to visit us,' one of the birth spirits said. 'Little Spot. Here she is!' said another.

'Oi! Can you hear us down there? Sprite's paid us a visit,' a loud one called to those closer to the overhang floor.

'I can't believe we get to see her so soon. I thought it would be a few lifetimes at least before we got close enough to talk,' cried another.

It felt pretty nice being surrounded and buried in them all. And I liked them a lot because they were motherless and waiting, just like me. 'Where do I sleep?' I asked them. 'I can't wait to be born. This is going to be fun.'

'Oh, you're not staying,' said one rudely as it pushed me down a bit.

'Yeah, just roll around. Enjoy yourself,' another quipped. 'Cause you won't be growing and moving with us.'

'Why—'

'Hey Sprite, I need to know, what colour is the harbour?' one blurted. 'I can't see anything from here.'

'Oh, and Sprite, is it true that when we get eyes, they will sting if we open them in saltwater? That's so weird.'

This set off a flood of questions. They tumbled out from birth spirits all through the mound. No one seemed interested in the answers. As soon as I tried to reply, I was immediately drowned out by another question. I tried to slow them down. To get them to tell me where I would be staying at least, but I gave up after a while. All I could do was listen as I slipped down.

'When I am born, I'm going to climb a hill. Is up a hard thing to do?'

'Have you ever seen legs? Bet they look ridiculous.'

'Tell me. What does moonlight smell like?'

'I can't wait to have teeth. Don't know why, but I want to bite something. Really hard!'

'Excuse me,' I said, worried I was slipping too close to the bottom. 'Will you hold me? I can't stop rolling down.'

'But down is where you're going, Sprite.'

'Down and out of the mound.'

'No!' I yelled. 'I want to go into a mum. I want to be born.' I tried to tense my sac, to spread out and take up room. But I kept sliding.

'Eel Mother said you'd do this.'

'We told her you'd freak out.'

'Have you met anyone who can breathe air?'

'When you get sunburned, should you peel off your skin?'

'Yeah, or let it flake away and watch a bird eat it for lunch?'

'Stop fighting, Sprite. Relax.'

'Yeah, relax. You've got ages yet.'

'Hold me please. Stop me from falling,' I begged. 'I want to stay.'

'You're not falling, silly. We're passing you around.'

'Give her to me. I want a go.'

'You're so lucky. I hope you know that, Sprite.'

'Too right, tiny Sprite. I'd give anything to be you.'

'Yeah, lucky last!'

'We'll probably live and die before you're even born.'

'Lucky little Sprite,' they all sang. 'The last of us to leave.'

'Imagine that! Living a whole life before Sprite gets a turn.'

'I can't,' said a little one. 'It makes me spin and feel yuck.'

Lucky last? I shrivelled myself. My sac went limp. I tried to pull away from the other eggs and block out their non-stop chattering.

Still, they shuffled and handed me about. So, I stopped trying to be anything then. What was the point? The birth spirits felt me withering. They tried to cheer me up.

'At least you don't have a lump squishing down on you all day.'

'Plus, you can feel things and see stuff. We can't!'

'Don't be sad, Sprite. You're different. Not like us.'

'Yeah, we're just babies.'

'Waiting to be born.'

I let everything go blurry and muffled then. I'm not sure how long it took me to move through them all. I didn't really care much. Eventually, I stilled and felt the warmth of the mound's base. The dumb birth spirits started saying their goodbyes.

'No offence, Sprite. We've got a system going.'

'Plus, it's squashy. No room here for you.'

'Go on, out you get.'

I was thrust from the mound into the waiting Eel Mother's body on the cave floor. Onto her only bony bit, no less. I thought about yelping because it hurt, and I wanted the birth spirits to feel guilty they had chucked me out, but I didn't bother. Eel Mother curled the tip of her tail around me. If I had eyelids they would have slid down and closed. And probably not opened again. Ever.

4.
Dreamtime Books

Ginny took two slow breaths. They pushed away the hint of Nath's Calvin Klein aftershave that was beginning to dance in her nostrils. She jumped from the stage, letting the shock of her heels on the bricks shake the final lingering whiff away. Without looking at the audience or hearing any of their gentle applause, she weaved through the maze of chairs and returned to the slatted table she'd left her bag on. Fabs was wrapping up, but no one was listening. She scooped up her bag and made her way towards the exit.

'Hey!' came a shout from behind.

Ginny started. Her words had created a lingering current that was quickly sucking her towards memories of him. She took in a steadying breath, focusing on the butt of a candle that flickered in its missing-brick pocket of wall. Settling, she turned slowly towards the voice.

A pixie-haired woman approached her. 'Thanks for your words,' she said, holding out her hand. 'Ginny, isn't it?'

'That's right,' Ginny said, surprised. She shook the woman's slender fingers.

'I'm Imogen, just a local.' She shrugged. 'I live in Mitchell Street.'

Ginny swallowed a smile.

'I enjoyed your poem,' Imogen said. 'Who are you under?'

'Sorry?' Ginny replied.

'Where do you study? Are you over at the uni?' Imogen asked.

'Nah,' Ginny replied, nose scrunched. She watched as Imogen's eyebrows rose into momentous escarpment ridges.

'You have a great grasp of metre and breath, so I thought ... but self-taught, that's pretty impressive.' She began rummaging through her deep, green leather bag. 'You're obviously well read. Who's your favourite poet? Ali Cobby Eckermann?' Imogen spoke quickly, snorting in frustration as she riffled through the bag.

Ginny could see she didn't really need to answer. So didn't.

'You're Koori, right?' Imogen added, still foraging. The further her arm disappeared, the louder her snorts became.

'I—'

'I work at a small publishing house, nothing big, but we're putting together an anthology early next year that I think your work could be good for.' Imogen finally retracted a crumpled, cream business card. 'Do you have an agent?' The woman stilled, waiting.

Upside down, Ginny read the card. *Commissioning Editor – Diversity and Inclusion.*

'There's no fee per se, all our poets will be invited to donate a piece. But it could lead to something in the future.' Imogen wiggled the card at Ginny's nose. 'With a bit of structural reinforcement, your poem could work really well. I think the concept of black love is something we all need to hear more of.'

'Tell me about it.' Ginny laughed. Sudden and heart-stopping, the image of Nathan smiling his cute half-smile in his sexy little knockout shorts flashed into Ginny's mind. 'But I've given up on it.' She shook her head, trying to dissolve him. Her shell earrings tinkled as they swung.

'You mustn't,' Imogen urged. 'Actually, I might—'

To thwart his magic, her own weakness and Imogen's weird apparition between the two, she blurted, 'I already have a publisher.'

'Oh, really? Who?'

'Dreamtime Books,' she said, straight and clear.

'Haven't heard of them,' Imogen said, returning the card into the handbag abyss. 'Are they Sydney-based too?'

'Kind of. They're helping me get some of my poetry out.' Ginny knew she had to be careful so continued, slowly. 'Just small runs in niche markets. Pretty lowkey. But they have deadly networks. And staunch leadership. I'm really happy with them.'

'That's good to hear, I must look them up. Would you have a contact? Maybe they'd be interested in some sort of mentorship or partnership.' Imogen resumed her rummaging, clambering for her card again.

'That's okay,' Ginny said. 'I'll just google you and cc you in an email. After I've asked if it's appropriate,' she said, eyebrow raised with a soft smile.

'Of course.' Imogen nodded. As she did, Ginny noticed a dainty tattoo behind Imogen's right ear. It was a book with flowing pages.

'It was great to yarn, Imogen.' She turned back towards the exit.

'Yes, to yarn,' Imogen giggled. 'And well done tonight. Seriously, Ginny. Keep at it,' she called.

Ginny raised her hand, already halfway out the door.

'And it'd be great to connect with your publisher,' Imogen yelled, 'when the time is right.'

'That'll be the twelfth of never, lady,' Ginny mumbled as she stepped onto the footpath outside. *Plus, your permanent ink pages were blank. You don't even warrant a meeting at this point.*

Hovering outside the entrance to the bookshop, a circle of young people approached, clicking at her.

'Black love.' They clacked. 'Propa deadly! Black love!' They snapped. 'Sick, sista. Sick. Hey, can we have a photo?'

Before she could refuse, one hand gripped her arm and pulled her into the cluster as another extended a phone.

'Hey sista, what's your handle? Don't forget to hashtag black love,' they gaggled. 'Yeah, black love, open mic. Add hashtag poetry slam somewhere too.'

'Don't get tangled up in gubba semantics, sista,' they continued. 'It'll guarantee you more likes.'

'But it wasn't a slam,' Ginny muttered.

'We just add it, for the likes.'

Shaking her head, Ginny left them grinning into their blue screen–lit palms.

Quickly, she was through the park and tunnel, and approaching the Smart Cookie Press poster again. Moving closer, Ginny imagined what it would actually be like to have a publisher. To have her ideas printed and taking root in the world. She drank in the poster's words … *an independent, student-run printing and publishing …*

The tree logo, bold and pronounced against its stark white background, thrust its trunk at her.

Ginny drew in a stream of growing coldness and held it in her chest and ribs. Something told her she needed to go to the tree and stand before it. So, instead of making her way towards the grimy bitumen back streets she was parked in, Ginny went left, finding the beginning of the sandstone pathway that snaked towards the Main Quad. Reaching the open square, she walked to the tree. In the evening light its presence took the form of the negative – its outline visible because of its commanding absence.

'Smart Cookie,' she spoke into the studied stillness as she approached. 'Ginny,' she said, coming to a halt at a protruding root. 'Great ... to meet you I guess?' Shrugging her shoulders, she reached through the silence and shadow, and placed her palm on the trunk of the tree. 'I'm – Dreamtime Books.' A flush pulsed from her fingertips. It flowed straight into her forehead. It flooded her follicles, making her hair stand on end.

Ginny inspected a cluster of drooping purple Jacaranda bells. Their heads were bowed, gesturing to the root-ripped, manicured green of the lawn. Her mind began to spark. She ran her eyes along the splayed system, creases mutating into wrinkled fingers, bulbous palms up, entreating.

'But I ain't a student.'

A cricket chirped, its irregular rhythm forcing her to concentrate.

'I don't know nothin about that kinda stuff.'

The insect jumped from the trunk of the tree onto its branch. Although light was almost non-existent, the flick caught Ginny's eye. She squinted into the treetops. Every bloom bowed at the roots below her.

'Well, maybe …'

The higher branches shimmied, their rustling filling the stone yard.

She reached into her handbag and brought out her notebook. She turned the red leather around in her hands then, fingering the pages, opened it. 'If they can—' Ginny traced the turrets and gargoyles of the sandstone building against the ageing night.

'Needs a bit of Blak love, by the looks.' Ginny scoffed as she tore at the poem. She jammed her heel into the woodchips at the base of the tree and pushed down hard. When she hit dirt, she scuffed a hole into it. Bending, Ginny placed the poem in the divot, then filled it in, treading on the soft soil and replacing the woodchips. She stood, head lowered over her freshly buried Blak love for a long while. The tinking of the cricket ceased. Clouds gathered then dissolved from the face of the beaming moon above her.

'Guess I'm published.' Ginny roused, turned her back to the tree and faced the Quad. 'Dreamtime Books,' she said in a full, echoing bellow. 'Choo!' The tail of the call cannoned around the stone square. Two purple bells rustled away from the branch and spiralled to the grass.

After a final tap of the new mound with the tip of her Cons, she left, making her way back to the car. By the time she arrived home and parked, threw her keys on the table and her bra on the floor, Ginny was well on the way to imagining what it would take for Dreamtime Books to root, to flourish. And grow.

5.

After the mound spat me out I got pretty low. I tried keeping to myself. That meant staying away from Eel Mother and her scratchy skin. But she could be pretty annoying when she wanted to be. And because she wanted to talk, she began poking and pushing me, trying to get me to speak.

'Sprite?' Eel Mother prodded.

I turned away. But because I looked the way I always did, she couldn't tell.

'Tell me, Sprite, what did you learn?'

'Eternity.' I collapsed my circle into a blob. Floppy and tired, like Eel Mother most probably was.

'You're sad,' she said to me. 'I understand.'

If a tear was only water and salt, I already knew about it.

Eel Mother took me up and raised me into a beam of light. It speared down from the above. She probably felt bad. I hoped she did. I wobbled on her tail. 'Apart from Great Whale, you, Sprite, are the one I've known longest in the world.'

Instead of that being a good thing, it made me feel a bit sick.

'I love you, Sprite,' she whispered.

'Sprite,' I sighed. 'Spot. The names of a nothing.' I tried melting into a puddly pool.

Eel Mother raised me to her. If we had noses, they would have touched.

'Maybe,' she said, stretching, her body tightening for a moment then flopping back to its regular sag, 'those birth babies showed you something important. What do you think that might be?'

She watched me intently, urging me to think. 'That I don't belong,' I huffed at her.

She shook her head. 'You know that's not true.'

'I don't care, Eel Mother.'

'Well, you should, Sprite.'

'Why? I'll be the last to go. That's what they said. The very last. There will be lifetimes, generations of lifetimes, to happen before I even get to be born.' I curled my imaginary shoulders from her. I slunk as low as an unborn birth spirit could. Eel Mother came so close to me that the water from her nostrils pushed on my sides and swirled me around until I faced her again.

She spoke slowly. 'My job is to leave those little ones in the places they will go into their mum. I have spent unending cycles inventing ways to take children to their mothers. It is my life's work. And I am grateful for it.' She looked directly into my eyes, even though I didn't have any yet. 'And you're right, Sprite. This will take a very long time.' Eel Mother held me to her. 'When the last of the spirits have been taken to their mothers,' she said as she shuffled, her voice softening and shaking a bit, 'and the mound gone, then you shall go into your mum. Your very own. One made especially for you. As you were made for her. The wait, Sprite, will be well worth it. I promise.'

She brushed her beak against me, then rose. Her body wagged as she swam into the harbour. I was pulled to the edge of her lair by her slipstream. Clusters of whiting and baby bream froze as she glided over them. After swimming a long, long way out, she turned, her body making itself into a humungous circle. This was when I saw her full length for the very first time. Her stretched-out sides began rippling. Bright colours then dark ones then sharp ones then faint. Her lights pushed into the water around the cove. Corals and shells and fish's stripes caught the rays and returned them tenfold. The cove lit up in majestic Eel Mother flashes.

The colours were beautiful. Everything was, now; I was certain I would be born.

On her return, Eel Mother slowed at the overhang entrance. The current twisted between her wrinkles and wobbling skin. 'Great Whale kissed you to me,' she explained, the skin under her eyes blushing silver then indigo.

Knew it, I thought.

'That's why things are different for you. It's why you are the last of the mound to go, my darling, dear little Sprite. And although you think it a very long time, it is only a flicker of what is to come.'

Her body drooped a bit. More lines appeared. The sudden thought of not being with her made me feel heavy.

'You will change it all, Sprite,' she said to me, the water from her breath turning me in my sac. 'Because you are everything.'

If I had a face I probably would have smiled. But I had no lips yet. Or teeth to pull them across. If I did, my smile would have been as wide as the harbour.

Eel Mother exploded into speckles and spots and lines. Each its own special colour. They surged and flooded her worn skin. 'Others are from Great Whale's spout. You,' she said as she wiggled, 'came from his lips. He made you with his kiss then rolled you down his backbone. Great Whale himself, Sprite! With a flick of his tail, he passed you to me. When all this …' She pushed out a silvery streak that reached every part of her watery realm. 'Was a stream.' She nudged me onto the nape of her neck. I lodged between two lines that lived on her there. 'It's time for you to earn your keep. You're going to help me place the spirits where they need to go.'

I swirled all over her, hugging her as best I could.

Eel Mother's body faded to its regular grey. She glided next to me, winding herself into coils. Her tail fanned air into the mound's tower. I flowed in the rhythm of Eel Mother's wave.

'If I'm going to help you and I have some questions along the way, will you answer them and not pretend you can't hear?'

'Eh?' she said, smiling. With her sides pulsing electric green she added, 'Sometimes, yes.'

'Will you let me poke myself out of the water to see parts of the above?'

'Once.'

'Will you introduce me to Great Whale if he comes by?'

Eel Mother stiffened a bit. Yellow flashes sprinkled across her cheek.

'Don't worry, I won't say anything about you being sweet on him.'

She snorted on me. It spun me around. Before I came to a stop I added, 'He probably knows anyway. Don't know if you noticed, Eel Mother, but you're not very good at hiding stuff.'

She swished a current over us all. I yawned, kinda. I had no mouth yet, but the bit of me where my face would go needed to stretch. Peace drifted into the mound. I filled my pretend lungs with imaginary air.

'I have to tell you something.' I was drifting.

'Mmm,' she murmured.

'The birth spirits asked me a question.'

'Go on,' she said, fanning. As she wafted, I felt myself and my words beginning to drift with the sleeping, creeping tide.

'"Does Eel Mother snore then choke on the water she sucks in?" they all asked. They really, really want to know.'

Her gills blew upon us, the water caressing our sacs, turning them. 'Your answer?' she said.

'I lied.' My egg flooded with stillness. In the cool of the current, I dissolved into the slow-forming sea.

6.

Proper Light

A robust bar of early winter light hit the end of Ginny's bed and crept its way up her sheets. She woke to its heat rousing the thin skin of her uncovered feet. Ginny wiggled her toes then rubbed one foot into its opposing arch. Wiping the sleep from her eyes, she curled towards the squat, lopsided, pine drawer she had liberated from a council clean-up. Ginny groped at its surface, knocking her notebook to the floor as she unplugged and picked up her phone. Opening Instagram, she tapped the search icon then navigated the cursor into its bar. She began typing, profiles instantly appearing as more letters were added. Ginny's thumbs froze at the appearance of the back of a head. She gazed, breath held, into its billowing, red hoodie. A slow exhale accompanied her inspection of the taut, toffee-skinned neck and the close, clippered shave with two tiger scratches just above the ear. She scoured the hair as it progressively lengthened, her smile at its tight, spiralling curls thwarted by a *tsk* at the plaited horsey dangling from the top of the crown. Ginny crept her thumb towards the profile. She baulked. A wave of warmth settled onto her shins. Their spiky hairs rose. She felt her pores expand as the hair speared out of the skin. The whole lower half of her body tingled. Holding the phone above her head, she closed her eyes for a moment, taking her mind to the fizzing skin and radiating warmth of her extremities. She welcomed the morning beam as it lay upon her. With her calf she rubbed its greeting into her opposing shin. She opened her eyes to witness wisps of skin particles billow into the shaft of sun. 'I've shed,' Ginny snorted, throwing her phone into the messy covers, and springing out of bed.

Ginny walked to the window, inspecting the bland, grey, extension blind. It fell well short of the bottom of the window frame. It came with the rental, and even though it was totally inadequate, her bond relied on it. This close to the window, warmth streamed in, resting on her thighs. She lifted the hem of her shapeless t-shirt, inviting the sunshine onto her entire thigh. 'I want this. Brightness. Sunlight,' she said, stretching her hands to the ceiling and rotating her shoulders till they cracked. From beneath the blind, she watched the legs of a woman, a blue half-lead with a trotting chocolate poodle on its end. A brown-booted torso-child on a pedal-less bike speared, quick time, along the street. Ginny turned from the window and faced her room. She looked at her phone. Its screen created a glow from amongst the sheets. 'Proper light,' she said. 'Not gammon stuff,' she added, flinging her hair forward and, in the same motion, taking up a hair tie from the tiled floor and shoving her hair into a loose bun. 'But today,' she said, scraping loose strands into the elastic, 'I'll settle for clean clothes.'

Ginny lurched forward and took up a pair of crumpled tights. A scrunched sock fell from inside one of the squashed legs. 'Don't think you're getting away,' she sang, swooping it up and shoving it back into the gathered fabric. 'From now on,' she said, scooping up a t-shirt bra in the far corner, 'sun on the bed on Saturday means washing. Not layin about wastin time.' Ginny fished out a yellow, lace G-string from under her bedside table. She shook her head as she jammed it into the growing bundle. 'Weekend sunshine will hereby be welcomed,' she proclaimed, swiping more crumpled clothes from the floor. 'Outdoor activity of my choosing on both Saturday and Sunday is a must!' She tossed a pair of jeans over her shoulder. 'The bed will be outlawed after nine am,' she said, punctuating the sentence with a pick and fling. 'Maybe ten, depending on the circumstance.' She continued gathering. 'And the phone,' she said, getting on her hands and knees near the head of the bed, 'is for food and transport only. Oh, and coffee.' Ginny yanked a scrap of dark grey fabric from under the corner of her bed. With her free hand she tossed the shirt, trying to make out its front. 'Yes! Knew you'd come back to me, Lizzo,' she cheered, smiling, and got to her feet again.

Beaming, Ginny walked the hefty, dirty pile into her kitchen and threw it into the drum of her washing machine. It was crammed into a pocket of space between the end of a long kitchen bench and her back door. Chucking in a handful of powder, she set the knob and clicked it on. Ginny easily found the drone and hummed back its note, accompanying the sound of water rushing into the vibrating machine. Feeling brave, she began playing with her notes as she slid along the tiles towards the bench's far corner. Ginny placed two pieces of bread in the toaster, clicking them down. Then, lifting the kettle and sloshing it around, she returned it to its base and flicked it on, emphasising her tap with a Beyoncé-esque run. She grimaced. 'Stick to what you know,' she said. 'My final weekend commandment.'

Ginny scuttled back to her bedroom and took up her worn notebook from the floor. A bulge near the back cover cradled the blue biro squeezed into its spine. Undoing the elastic strap, she flicked through the pages. Scribbles and highlights and arrows and stars flicked past, each squiggle drawing attention to a line or word or thought. The volume thinned beneath her thumb. 'Could be worse,' she said, chucking the book down and putting her toast on a plate. She buttered it, making sure to create two grease-glinting pools. She then peeled and dissected a banana. Ginny placed the thin curves on top. 'Might be some stuff worth editing,' she reasoned, pouring the now boiled water into a mug holding a waiting teabag. Ginny sloshed some milk in the mug and added two teaspoons of sugar and stirred, jangling the teaspoon against the mug's sides. Tucking the notebook under her arm, she walked her sweet tea and banana toast to the front door. Opening it, she plonked herself on her top step directly in a ray of light. A pair of kookaburras chortled as she squinted into the brightness. Ginny set her crockery down and drew her knees to her, making a surface for the notebook to rest on. She licked her index finger then turned the pages, blowing escaping strands of hair from her forehead as she scanned and read. She circled the pages she thought showed promise. Flicking back and forth, she counted them. 'See that?' she called to the birds. 'Seven of em. Ha!' she laughed. 'Seven poems. Seven sisters.' The jaunty revolution of a new laugh filled the street. 'They were trying to be rid of a bloke too.' The bird's laugh broke, its climbing pulse stalling then dissolving into the day. Ginny listened as the echo travelled down the bitumen and flooded the street's end. 'Guess that's what happens when you bring Dreamtime into the equation.' She put down the book, sipped and smiled into her steaming tea.

Reducing her breakfast to a few crumbs and backwash, she whipped round the lounge and straightened the bathroom. Afterwards, Ginny took a whiteboard marker and wrote the list of poems directly onto her bedroom window. There, just below the reach of the blind, the sun could wake them every morning. The titles would then write themselves onto her skin. The thought pleased her so much that she didn't bat an eyelid when she found a pair of Nath's Calvin Klein's in the bottom of the wash. She pegged them out on the clotheshorse at the opposite end to her own underwear. When they were dry, she planned on taking them to the Salvos bin and hurling them into its waiting red abyss.

7.

I had no idea how huge the harbour was. There were
coves and caves galore. Inlets and estuaries I'd never
known of. Pockets of secrets everywhere. Even though
everything was basically just water and sand, every part of
that place was different. And beautiful. In its own way. As
Eel Mother spat or hoicked or wafted spirits into mums, she
left me to notice all the slopes and banks and holes. And the
angle of sun and patterns of wave and wash and shadow and
sand. How water met rock was always awesome. And how
boulders crumbled into sand was madness. I started to notice
the different colour of every grain of sand. Eel Mother said
this change happened in the above too. Southern harbour
grains were mostly orange, but north-side sand was a blazing
yellow like how I imagined a flower to be. But that was just
a guess since I didn't know a thing about flowers. Or any
above thing, really.

Eel Mother told me my job was to jam birth spirits into her. When she nudged the bottom of the mound I would have to be ready. The gentlest bump spilled spirits all over the place! I was responsible for shoving them onto her floaty-waiting body before any of them rolled away. I got great at it. Pushing them into every Eel Mother crevice. Between folds of skin, plugged into wrinkles. Under fins, behind teeth and tucked into gills. I jammed them in hard. I had big problems lifting her skin up and shifting her blubber and stuff. But I had to, to find enough droopy bits and skin pockets – big enough to shove spirits into but light enough not to crush or splat them. Sometimes, I would have to tickle her a bit so her skin would tighten just enough to slide a couple more in somewhere. I liked those times – where work and fun were basically the same thing.

Whenever I got impatient and thought about making things go quicker, I reminded myself that getting ready to be born was a big thing. It might make the birth spirits worried if I was rough and hurrying them. And I wanted them to feel happy. It was a special time for them, and they were my friends after all. I also knew they were weak and slippery and would just slide out or fall off if I didn't do my job properly. I wanted to make sure they all got into a mum. The way Eel Mother would do for me one day. I figured all the pushing and shoving would make me pretty strong and that would end up being a good thing. Even though I didn't have them, my arms and legs ached from all the work she had me doing.

Eel Mother's glide was always extra sleek coming home after spirit placing. In those slow, tired times, she'd speak about wondrous things. She taught me of the moon and showed me how it made the waters swell. She made me watch how it affected different creatures. And spoke of the ways it marked movement in the above. I used to think the moon only pushed darkness into the harbour. But Eel Mother showed me that it spread a softer kind of light. A glowy, playful, buried sort of one. A pulsey one that focused things into clusters. That lit up parts while letting other stuff fade. I loved it. Moonlight in the harbour made things magical. I got so full of ideas of the moon it made me a bit angry that I hadn't seen it yet, although I'd been asking Eel Mother for ages. Instead of boosting me up to see it, she described it to me from beneath the waves. She said it always smiled, although sometimes the smile was shy. And that when I could see it for myself, it would make me feel warm inside. But it would probably mean the land was cold. I didn't get that part. But I liked how it sounded all the same.

She explained how the above worked a little bit too. Air was basically the same as water, she said. It was also food. Up there, stuff like trees and animals and people and plants, in fact everything in the above, needed it. They sucked air in and let it out, just like we did with water. But air wasn't heavy or thick the way water was. It was thin, so things spread out. Sometimes air was really hot. Other times it was colder than the coldest current. And nothing ever floated in the air unless it was light. Really, really light.

Lighter than air, they'd say in the above, she told me.

Even birds, stingrays of the sky, had to hold themselves up and push themselves through it.

'It's different up there, Sprite. The above is always pulling things down,' Eel Mother said to me. I must have looked frightened cause she added, 'But when you feel that, you know you're alive.'

Waving past a shoal of flowy seaweed, I shifted on the brow of her beak.

'Tell me more, Eel Mother,' I asked.

'You can try and prepare for it, Sprite,' she told me. 'But the above makes most sense when you just go for it. Let things land where they may, so to speak. Try to remember what it's like down here. It will help you in the above. There's little use in fighting the flow. The same goes for up there.' She prodded her beak at the above. Her gill flaps shook. 'Forcing, Sprite, only makes heavy things push down harder.'

If this job ever ended, I was going to miss Eel Mother when I left. Big time.

'Eel Mother,' I asked once, 'Will I bring everything with me after I get into a mum and she makes me born? Memories and lessons and stuff?'

She slowed, her wagging holding us in place. Placing me onto her back, craning her head to face me. She flickered deep blue and dark, moss green with winking purple specks. I looked at her white eyes, perfect black beads in their centres. She stayed silent. We bobbed as the current shifted around us.

'Will I remember you?'

Her eyes widened. Her nose feelers flared. I panicked, thinking I had jammed a spirit in too deep and we had forgotten to place it and it was listening to us and beginning to stress out. She let her bottom jaw droop. A poddy mullet swam in and sucked at a crooked bottom tooth.

'When you have a mum, her hands will be your sand. And you'll know them the way you know this place.' She turned her head. The mullet took off. 'All mothers protect in the best ways they know. They hold and hug and make sure their little ones are safe. They are their little ones' shells, but soft.' Her voice lowered. 'Whether you remember details or not, little Sprite, you can be sure every part of you has been drenched in love. It is a wondrous happening. Its force shapes the entire world.'

She arched her back and guided me along her spine and back onto her head. I felt Eel Mother's backbone wag against the water, moving us forward again. 'Mothers are experts at overflow, Sprite.'

'What do you mean?'

'You thirst. They fill. You become hungry, they fill you again. And so it goes. Drinking and filling, needing, receiving – an endless stream. Soon thirst and want disappear. Then it becomes a never-ending pour of goodness, from her into you.'

I looked at Eel Mother, she was staring into the cove as she glistened apricot flecks.

'You may forget every word or kiss or gift, but that doesn't mean they weren't given. It all goes into the vessel.' She nodded at my soul egg. 'That's what a body is for, as much as I can make out. It takes in air and makes breath. Eats food and makes movement. Takes ideas and creates art. Things go in and become wonderful. And those wonderful things are expelled in the most magnificent ways. We don't need to remember everything poured into us. But we can be thankful it happened.' Eel Mother's scales ignited in a flash of every imaginable colour. Just as quickly, the rippling rainbow disappeared. 'When it comes to families and parents and breath and the above, Sprite, it's all about living it. Not about remembering so much.'

A tremor rushed through my egg. It might have been love. Flooding in. Or connection or belonging beginning to grow. Whatever it was, I let it swirl around inside. I was grateful it was there. It stayed warm and tingly until we got back to the ledge of the lair. Eel Mother made herself into a coil then motioned me to nestle beside her. We gazed at the shimmering above. The grinning moon placed silver plates between the water's hands.

I brushed into her.

'Do I work you too hard, little Sprite?' She contracted, pulling me to her.

I felt her hug then shrugged my reply.

She laughed a little. The giggle was tiny, but it shook her whole body. Eel Mother took in a full and deep breath.

'You and I, two grains of sand on the ocean floor,' she said. The words floated around us, their peace a spoken dream.

'What does that mean?' I said, yawning, kind of.

'Only that you can be something and nothing at the same time,' she whispered.

I was so calm, so content in her coils, I was nearly gone. She shifted me a little as she rested her head on the cave floor. She was soft. I dissolved into the closeness.

'I'll always remember you, Sprite,' I heard her say before I dissolved into salt.

Stillness flooded my shell. I tried to answer but my inside trailed off, overtaken by the ebb of the moon and cove's tide.

8.
Wormbow Serpent

A worm, glistening and thin, had somehow snuggled into a trough of absent putty in Ginny's kitchen window. It stretched snug against the glass, the pristine wrinkles of its tapered head sometimes extending against the pane, mimicking the final, frantic descents of dribbling droplets of rain on the glass outside. She had only noticed it after flicking on the kettle, seeking a break from a concentrated stint of editing. Muscles stiff and eyes stale, Ginny had risen from the couch and unwound herself from her nest of favourite throw and familiar, lumpy cushions to make herself a well-earned sachet cappuccino. Waiting for the water to boil, she spotted it and immediately began piecing together the worm's most probable route. It could only have come from the unloved spider plant plonked a third of the way up her outdoor, concrete stairs. The pot plant belonged to the tenant beneath her – a short, dark-haired girl who Ginny rarely, if ever, saw.

Ginny fancied the excessive rain had flooded the worm from the safety of its dry potting mix, forcing it over the edge and onto the step. From there it must have wriggled up the rest of the flight of stairs, slid under her door and foisted itself onto her sink and then the windowsill. Either that or it fell from the mouth of a bird. It couldn't have come from inside her flat. The only plant she had was in the bathroom. And that was plastic – a dusty, gammon dollar gum she had liberated from the alleyway behind her block months ago. So, stairs or beak it must have been. As the kettle boiled, molecules of steam curled towards the worm. Ginny flicked the kettle's latch then moved it away from the window. She ripped the sachet open with her teeth and dumped the shimmering granules into her waiting mug. 'I'd offer you one but, y'know, that'd just make me a murderer. Scalded to death by whatever this is,' she said, flapping the empty packet and tossing it on the bench. 'That's not a fitting way to go after what you've been through. Mighty worm. Wormbow serpent,' she added, laughing hard into the dull chrome taps. Ginny picked up a spoon and stirred the hot sludge, then blew into its growing foam. She leaned in and inspected the creature. Rather than a coating of slime, the worm's skin shone translucent orange-pink. It contracted, a ripple surging along its slender length. 'You're a bit of a stunner,' she said. The worm lifted its front end and stretched into the air. Ginny took a shallow sip of her steaming concoction. The heat hitting her lips made her scrunch her face. 'Not sure if a windowsill's a good long-term plan, though. Rarely is, for anyone.' She tried another sip, this time copping a heap of sugary powder at the back of her throat. She coughed. 'Tell you what,' she continued, wiping her eyes, 'if you're still here after I knock off these last few pages, we'll go for a walk.' Ginny turned from the sink. 'Just me and my new best friend.' She began walking back to the couch. 'A spineless dirtbag. No offence,' she yelled over her shoulder. 'Seems I have a type.'

An hour later, Ginny placed the final full stop at the end of the passage and shoved the biro into her pigtail bun. She wiped the tears from her cheek and ran her nose along the wrist of her grey jumper. She blew a sigh into the middle of the lounge room, then rubbed the back of her neck, stretching the muscles as she kneaded them. Unfurling herself from the throw and the lounge, Ginny stood. Crushed balls of paper fell from her lap and onto the rug. She looked at them and sniffled. 'And to think I almost didn't live at all.'

She kicked the paper balls out of the way as she slid into the bedroom, her woolly bed socks scuffing against the cold tiles. It was still raining. She slid her feet into a pair of soiled, green rainboots that were plonked at the foot of the bedroom door. Their feel lifted her spirits. Ginny always enjoyed the adventures she had in them. She reached for the raincoat slung over a chest of drawers, wiggled her thick, jumpered arms into it and clasped the zipper. Returning to the couch she took up her notebook and placed it in the inside pocket of the raincoat. Ginny pulled the magenta zip all the way up as she walked into the kitchen, continuing the motion even as she swiped an empty, unopened envelope from the table. 'Your chariot awaits, little worm, if you're still with us.' She examined the windowsill. The worm remained, still stretched along the glass. It was motionless. Ginny blew a soft stream of air onto the body of the creature. It didn't move. Moving closer still, Ginny pulled the biro from her hair, removed its lid and slid its tip under the centre of the worm's body. Its head lifted, then its body contracted, sending a quiver down its entire length. 'Yes!' she said, scooping it carefully onto the tip of the pen and shaking it into the envelope. 'Let's get going. The rain will bring us back to ourselves,' she said, folding the top of the broken envelope and sliding it into her pant pocket. Ginny descended the stairs with the worm tucked away safely. On her way down, she checked out the spider plant. The small pile of dirt in the bottom of the pot was soggy. 'Don't blame you,' Ginny said, continuing down and into the street. She smiled as the rain popped on the hood of her raincoat. She smiled even harder as she danced around drippings of people – impatient scurriers – tiptoeing over puddles, skirting around trickling drains and dodging gushing bus tyres as they whirred past. For Ginny, rain brought a concentrated energy to the world. It made things close. And meaningful. She walked towards the library, listening to the sound of her feet on the pavement, the huff of her breath in her collar. Approaching the last street before the building's high awning, Ginny heard her blood pulsing and felt its hum in her ears. Slowing near the library's sprawling, and deserted, outdoor café, she felt beads of sweat tingle on her top lip. A drizzle descended from a pool that had formed in the small of her back. Ginny giggled. She didn't mind. She loved sweating in the rain. She didn't know why but she reckoned her sweat and falling rain were relatives. Cousins, most probably. 'It's always wins, Worm,' Ginny said, clumping over the slate tiling and towards the elaborate top garden that framed the library's opening. 'In the battle between rain and human, water takes it out every time.' She reached into her pocket and with great care removed the envelope. Water splattered on the back of her hand. 'You know better than most, there'll always be a crack to wriggle into.'

Ginny peeked into the envelope's fold. The worm stretched towards the gush of fresh air. She winked then, looking around, walked down the rampway towards a second garden bed. It was filled with clumps of elegant grasses, droplets of water hanging suspended from bowed stems. A vibrant Kangaroo Paw burst furry, red flowerheads into the grey surrounds. Ginny made her way towards it, then kneeled on the concrete lip of its bed. Bending close, she opened the envelope and shook the worm into the dirt at the plant's base. After a complete rotation, the worm stilled beside the fanning green base. Ginny watched. The worm stayed limp, still. 'This'll be a perfect home for you,' she said. 'Better than my hovel. And if you miss me, I'm only a bus ride away. I know how independent you are.' As if on cue, a thick, blue vehicle – its windows fogged and precipitating – squirted dirty, city gutter water over the footpath behind them. 'See, the bus stop's just there.' Ginny came closer. The worm stayed still. 'Are you angry with me?' she said, bowing down further, her nose almost in the dirt with it. Ginny placed the envelope on the soil beside them. 'I'll come and visit. Promise. I'm at the library a lot.' This seemed to rouse the worm. It began contracting its sleek body, moving slightly towards the bright white paper. 'There you go,' she added. 'The coffee's okay, but stay away from the ham and cheese croissants. Too greasy.' The worm, slinking steadily now, lodged its front half back on the envelope. 'Unfortunately,' Ginny said, 'I'm not cleared for pets.'

The worm arched its back and inched along the envelope. The rain and larger drops from the tips of the grass smacked into the paper. Ginny watched as the worm separated a soggy scrap from the paper's fold then speared it into the soil, covering it completely. When it finished, the worm extended its body as high as it could towards Ginny's face. She stared at the worm. She felt dribbles of rain hit her ankle and ooze under her sock. The worm stretched out again. 'What? This?' Ginny unzipped the top of her raincoat and pulled out her notebook.

The worm started bobbing.

'But this was just for me. To make sense of.'

The worm went crazy, zigzagging up and down then sideways.

'But it's not good enough,' Ginny said, opening the notebook. 'I wasn't … enough.' Ginny stared at the neat letters and uniform spacing of her latest entry. A droplet hit the centre of the paper. Blue ink began to run. With one eye on the worm, Ginny's fingers moved to the top of the page and pulled. Worm wiggled from the edge of the envelope and followed Ginny's hand as she placed the paper in the dirt. Coming to its edge, the worm extended its whole body into the air, waving its head and neck coils in a circle before spearing into the ground. As it landed, an army of worms burrowed up to the surface and engulfed the page. Worm and water and soil dissolved Ginny's finely crafted words, making short work of the paper, reducing it to insignificant specks of white in a sea of soil.

Ginny stood, her writing and the worm gone. From the rampway there was nothing to say anything at all had happened – no slime trail, no disturbed dirt, no scrap of paper, or word of a poem to bear witness. Ginny raised her face to the sky wondering if she too might be broken down and dissolved and disappeared. She invited the water to pool in her eye sockets. She then opened and blinked the falling water in. The sting of cold made her own eyes water warm salt. Streams ran down her face then onto her skin under the neck of her jumper. Electrified with impermanence, and now armed with newfound worm wisdom, Ginny knew exactly what it was she must do.

9.

Round thuds smacked upon the water. A sound began to ping. I could hear it from the back of Eel Mother's cave. I looked to the mound to see if it had woken any of the birth spirits. I would have loved for one to come out to the rock ledge and watch what was happening with me. Maybe frolic a little bit. Pretend to push me from the ledge and into the current. But they were all bound together. None of them moved without Eel Mother's say-so. Plus, they were asleep. The soft browns and shy yellows and faint oranges that rippled through the mound told me so.

Eel Mother was tan brown and sleeping too. Breathing deeply, her skin sags were flapping in the current. Baby mulloway nibbled the scum from her gills.

I nudged away from Eel Mother's side and down the lair tunnel. Our watery roof was dimly in a hazy, mushed-up kind of way. The freshness of the rain made a layer of blur just below the surface. It reminded me of the squirts Eel Mother blew out her gills when she was sighing or drawing a story or bringing a memory back to life.

I watched the tiny droplets thwack. It hurt my head part to think of something falling with such force. I couldn't imagine the above just then, all air and water and weighed down, dropping things. So, I concentrated on the patterns. Each droplet created a splash that washed into another. Ripples arrived and fanned outward, creating a churn. But it wasn't like the chop of regular no-rain time. It was jerkish. Large drops pushed into the water and turned into round bubble bums on the surface. Just as quickly they bounced away. Bubbles are always hilarious cause they usually follow a surprise. They make me laugh every time.

At the edge of the lair, I had a thought that rain blobs were probably the way the harbour replaced the space that birth spirits left behind when they were sent to a mum. It made total sense to me. Lifetimes of spirit eggs had left the water. Their spreading was constant. For sure the harbour would need to be topped up. Maybe that's why Eel Mother said the harbour was a creek once. Cause they hadn't got the system right. Or maybe there was a drought and no rain fell to replace birth spirit space. Maybe she had worked too fast and spread too many of them too quickly and that made the water level fall.

I looked up at the rain. 'Thanks,' I told it. 'Keep it coming if you can. We've been shifting heaps of the little—'

Eel Mother slithered up behind me and shoved me off the ledge.

I tumbled. Turquoise flared from her skin and across the basin. She always flashed it whenever she felt cheeky. Or playful. She let me fall. She always did. She thought it was scary for me. I'd never told her I couldn't wait to be drifting on my own someday.

'Rain, Sprite!' she yelled from the cave.

'Isn't it beautiful?' I called back.

'It is, little Sprite. You will earn your keep today! Rain makes everything fizz.' Her chuckle pulsed through the inlet. It frightened two puffer fish back into the sea grass.

Instead of sucking me back like she normally did, Eel Mother slid down to meet me, wiggling her old body hard down to the sea floor. Pulling up just before the bottom, she made herself into a set of coils so I was perfectly positioned to be squished into her middle.

This is gunna hurt, I thought, holding my non-existent breath, waiting to be smothered in fat rings. But she folded her soft body around me.

With me in her middle, Eel Mother tensed herself into a hard circle. Her constriction made a vacuum of her tightening coils. Water pushed up from the circle and I rocketed upwards.

'And away you go!' She laughed.

I rushed past the lair, swirling through the blue. I didn't stop. The force of Eel Mother's spout had me breaking the surface. Drops of rain cannoned towards the sea as I shot through them. I copped a few as I exploded past. I was an upside-down raindrop. Or a back-to-front one. I couldn't work out which. Whatever I was I felt incredible soaring through air. I got an awesome view of the harbour. As much as my unmade eyeballs could see anyway. And the beach and the trees and sky and other above stuff looked so cool. When I stopped rising and began to fall, it was the same fun but in reverse.

I tried to race the raindrops to see who could whack the water first. But it was kinda unfair cause I had come from a great squirt of an ageless eel and knew all about the water and what was beneath it. And a bit about the above now too. But they knew nothing and cared even less about stuff. I burned them all. No contest. I could have gone up and back in the time they took to plop, dumb and weightless, into the sea.

I sank past the raindrops and through the sweet water haze back to Eel Mother.

'C'mon, Sprite,' she said impatiently. 'We've got things to do.' She nudged the mound with her beak bit. Drowsy birth spirits started shooting all over the place.

She stared hard at me. 'Haven't lost one yet, Sprite. And I'm not going to, am I?'

'No, Eel Mother,' I chimed back as I shovelled a heap inside her nose.

'And why won't I?' she asked, twitching the spirits into comfortable spots inside her nose spaces.

'Because everyone is precious,' I sang, corralling as many birth spirits as I could from the front of the avalanche.

'Will it be harder for them, Eel Mother … you know … with all that, going on up there?' I whispered as I bundled birth spirits into a crinkle near her ear hole. I didn't want any of them to worry, it made them wiggle and fidget too much.

'Oh,' she sang back. 'That's right. I haven't told you the rule. Rain makes things much more exciting, Sprite.' A ripple went through the spirits. The whole cove began to tingle.

Eel Mother motioned for me to lodge myself into my favourite spot, a cosyish wrinkle in the middle of her forehead. As I squished in, she inhaled an endless gush of birth spirits. She must have sucked in a trazillion of them. As they gushed inside, I heard them squealing. It delighted them. Because I was a bit jealous, I hoped her crookedy jaws might squash a few. But they weren't, of course. And I was only half hoping. With a powerful swish, we burst from the overhang and into open water.

Eel Mother didn't slow until we reached the shallows of a wide, bright beach. Tilting her head, she let me fall from her and plop into the golden sand a short distance away.

She gave me a wink once I was settled. Then she flicked her tail and rose like a jet, punching the surface of the water.

Half her body lifted out. I knew cause I was pulled to the surface by her slipstream and bobbled, half floating, half submerged myself. Through the rain I watched Eel Mother fizz herself in a spinning upwards spiral. As she ascended, she snapped back her head then whipped it forward. Spirits flung from her mouth and body in every direction, spreading into every crevice of the cove.

Then, a huge raindrop whacked into me and shoved me back to the beach bottom. I listened to the rain's continuing plops as I skipped against the sand. Grains crunched and shifted as I slid amongst them. In the wake of Eel Mother and creation's greatness, I felt every bit an unborn nothing.

Eventually Eel Mother joined me on the sand. Free of birth spirits, yellow flecks sparked from her dark sag.

'Did you see, Sprite?' Her gills and nose holes flared. I could tell she was buzzing, electrified.

I nodded. I didn't want her to know how I really felt. A bit sad. And jealous. But most of all alone.

She wafted over me and swallowed me into a now vacant belly roll. Her muscles passed me into a large fold near the top of her spine. I felt her soften as she cradled me there.

In silence she turned and began wiggling back to her lair. As she moved, Eel Mother shot silver flashes and green streaks and bursts of red along her body into the water. Prawns and fish and tiny little crabs darted away and under things as we moved overhead. Her strobing created pools of coloured rain ripples. She popped me out of her fold a bit so I could see. I would have thought it wonderful if I wasn't so meaningless.

Eel Mother swam into a warm patch of water. She lingered in it, swishing her tail just enough to keep us hovering in place.

She released a fold of skin. 'You okay, Sprite?'

I couldn't make an answer just then. There was a hitch in my throat bit. It felt hard. And closed.

She kept squiggling, holding us in the heated flow. A grouper lumbered past. His enormous head bulge was yuck.

Most of the birth spirits would be inside their mums by now.

'You don't like being stuck with me, do you?' Eel Mother asked.

I stared at the grouper's down-turned lip. It made him look grumpy as well as gross.

'I love you,' was my honest, empty, woeful reply.

'But you would love a proper mother more.' Her body went tight. I knew it was a hug, Eel Mother style.

I nodded. As much as a blob could.

'I understand.'

The grouper squeezed out a cloud of poop. He swished it towards us then darted into the green.

'When will the mound get smaller, Eel Mother?' I asked, securing myself into a line on the other side of her body away from the wafting grossness.

'Over aeons and surges, cycles and tides, the mound has always been the same.' She stared at the rocks and grasses and seaweed. 'This is how things should always be.' Electricity clicked inside her body meat.

The centre of my egg sac contorted. It made me dizzy. I began to shiver – how I don't know. 'But you said, I will be the last to go. So, it has to start shrinking. Otherwise I'll—' Dim plops of rain overtook the silence.

Eel Mother continued swimming, her body's repeating curves waving us on. The rain continued. Bubbles and plops spackled the surface. At the rock overhang, Eel Mother released me. She coiled, adjusting so I was in the centre of her black pin-pupils. 'A powerful mother awaits you, Sprite. I promise.' A golden flash ran down her sides. 'She is strong. Do your best to be just like her.' Eel Mother nudged me with her beak then snorted on me. Her warm inside waters settled me a little. She took me into her flab. 'You will come into your mother, Sprite, have no fear of that. She will be a force. She will have to be. For she will be mother in a time hardest to be one.'

The rain from the above eased into a patter. It sprinkled against the surface, making it look like specks of sand rather than rain.

'How I will love her, Eel Mother.' I snuggled into her folds. 'I already do.'

She brought her tail close and fanned me. 'I know, Sprite.'

'And will we be happy together? My mum and me?'

The rain overhead stopped. The cove became still. 'For the time it takes to live a life, you will.'

From the cusp of her lair, I watched schools of fish dart in the patches of newly sweet sea. I tried relaxing into Eel Mother's folds. But she felt scratchy, and I found it hard to settle. Mostly because I had no way of making out what a mother looked like, or how long a life should be.

10.
Downstream

Ginny kicked off her thongs and walked onto the weir. The sharp, angry stones mixed through the cement hurt her heels. As soon as she could, she sidled onto a submerged step, taking extra care as she inched across its thin layer of moss. The ledge led to an opening, a narrow concrete fishway that allowed the bodies of water to connect despite its concrete barrier. Carefully she stepped into its channelled flow.

Cool waters ran downstream and into the wider half of the creek. It was, for the most part, warm, but pockets of freshness stroked her feet, tickling the hair on both big toes. Steadying, Ginny placed the shopping bag of ragged empty bottles onto the concrete.

Before filling them, she bent into the flowing water and plucked out a plastic food container lid and a sheet of polystyrene. Ginny chucked them onto the bank. The effects of the recent downpour clung to the creek. The rain had dressed the usually murky water in a scum of pollen and floating debris. Dirty plastic ghosts hovered in the She Oak branches at the high-water mark. A shredded pair of pyjama pants sprawled next to the weir. Takeaway coffee cups and styrofoam packaging and play-pen plastic balls meandered on the still surface. A brown duck paddled deftly, avoiding them while wading into the narrow upstream. Ginny unscrewed the lid of the first bottle and submerged it.

The city is the grot, she thought, *not you*. Ginny watched bubbles of air galumph from the bottle's lip. When one was full, she took out the next, repeating the action, filling each of the remaining five. When done and arranged side by side, the bottles glinted with brookish, butter-brown water. Its winking amber clarity urged Ginny's hand into the current. She brought her wet fingers to her lips. *Huh? Thought this was a saltwater place.* She dipped her hand in, tasting again. The wetness was lukewarm. And fresh. It opened her palate. Softened her jaw. 'Thanks,' she said, wiggling her toes. 'You know,' she went on, 'for staying fresh amongst all the trash.'

Ginny straightened then gazed downstream. A supermarket trolley rose from a dumping of sandstone boulders. The fish ladder's current ran straight towards it. 'And sorry,' she sighed. 'We're crappy guests,' she said, approaching lowness.

A crow that had picked its way along the concrete hopped towards the collection of bottles. Twitching, it pecked at one, then looked up at Ginny.

'But this publisher will regenerate the ecology.' She straightened. 'Enhance the environment. Dreamtime Books thanks you,' she added, 'for your generous help with my, *our*, first publication.'

The bird hopped to the shoreline, its talons tapping against the cement as it moved. Ginny loaded the bottles into the green bag and pulled herself out of the current. She swung the weighty bag onto one shoulder, stepped into her thongs and drove home.

11.

El Mother wiggled me about, rousing me from my liquid rest.

'C'mon, Sprite.' She jiggled. 'Great things feel like they will happen today.'

'Oh yeah?' I stretched in my sac. 'Like what? Every day's a bit the same to me, if I'm honest.' She had me working too hard.

'C'mon, get moving.'

She nudged the mound and slunk backwards. A wave of birth spirits spilled out, dislodging from the towering mass. I moved fast, well-practised, packing them into crevices, shoving them into wrinkles and smoothing them into lines that hung all over her. After heaps of jamming and shoving, Eel Mother nudged me onto the top of her head. I settled into the two folds of her scowl line.

Eel Mother surged past the cave entrance and over the small collections of rocks and seaweed that lingered there. Almost every time we exited the cave and swam into the open harbour, the birth spirits were deadly quiet. Probably because it was the first time they got to see anything of the world. Even the one they were about to leave. I used to try and imagine how I'd feel going into a mum. I was pretty sure I'd be nervous. All bippy and jumpy inside. Probably quiet as well.

This batch were so stunned, all I could hear was the swoosh of Eel Mother's tail as it propelled us forward. Eel Mother hummed as she swayed. But the hum wasn't a sound. It was beats and flashes of unfolding colour. This song started dark but gradually got lighter until her whole body shone silver, iridescent lines of colour cannoning down her sides.

We swam for an age, moving into odd waters. Even though I had no mouth, I knew the taste of this place was different. Sweet, sort of. The water shrunk closer and the banks tapered in, funnelling us into a shallow, muddy channel.

'Isn't it beautiful, Sprite?'

'It's different,' I said as a wall of rock emerged from the murk in front of us. 'Where are we, anyway?'

'Almost the end of the line.' She laughed.

I heard a little birth spirit whimper then.

'My beauties,' she said, curving into a kind, soft half-circle. 'You are very lucky to have mums that live in this place. Great Whale sent me a message to bring you here,' she announced.

'He did?' I whispered.

A pink streak flashed, just beneath her jaw.

'He sent a song into the harbour about it. And now ...' She flicked her bulk and swung herself completely around. 'Here you all are. About to go into a mother.'

My roundness bubbled and flexed a little. 'Why are they so special? And why do they get to be born here?' My questions came out shouty. Almost a yell.

Eel Mother smiled. 'High country,' she replied, shimmering.

'What's so good about that?' I sounded rude. I knew it. But I had a right to be. I'd been working my bubble off while others got all the perks. I also had no idea what high country really even was.

Eel Mother shook me from her head. Hard. 'Too many questions.'

I bobbled into the muddy bottom. She flopped her belly fat over me as she swam towards the stone wall. 'And too much talk.' Lining her great body along the bottom of the rock, she waited for me to emerge. 'This is where I do my greatest work, Sprite.' A lilac flash came over her head. 'If I do say so myself.'

'Eel Mother?' shivered one lone voice from within a fold. 'That rock looks huge. Much bigger than your overhang and nothing like the cove boulders we've come from. You won't smash us into it, will you?'

'And there are mums waiting for us close by, right?' whimpered another. 'It's a bit scary out here.'

Panic rippled through the birth spirits. Eel Mother's bulk jerked with the sniffles and sobs and sharp in-breaths.

Then one cried out, 'Will you take me back, Sprite?'

'Yes, me too. Please. I'm not ready for this.'

'Me neither, maybe next tide is better.'

Soon most of the birth spirits began to plead, mostly with me, to save them.

'Do something, Sprite. Eel Mother might have gone mad.'

'Tell her to go back, Sprite. We'll go back on top of the pile. We don't mind.'

'Yeah,' sniffed another. 'We wanna go home.'

I didn't get a chance to reply. Eel Mother lifted her body. 'And so you shall,' she said.

In an instant Eel Mother was pointing skyward, propelling herself as fast as she could. Her jagged bottom teeth burst through the water first. Her slipstream sucked me to the surface. Again. I swayed in the churn just enough to see it all. The entire length of Eel Mother extended out of the water and into the above. Her power lifted her parallel to the towering escarpment that rose at the river's end. Suspended higher than the tallest piece of rock, Eel Mother shook herself, spinning birth spirits on top of and past the cliff.

I bobbled back to the bottom of the river, waiting for the thwack of her saggy body hitting the surface. But she entered without a splash. Her return was so smooth she glided back without a sound.

She nestled. Then giggled. Mud squelched from beneath her belly fat. The gooeyness of it made her chuckle some more. Her fins swished in the sludge. 'I feel young again, Sprite. Almost a child myself!'

Even though I was only a circle, an empty, unmade, unowned egg sac, I was all wide eyes and open mouth.

'Why so amazed?' she nudged.

'You went so high.'

'Naturally,' she replied, encouraging muddy brownness to ooze from beneath her chin. 'How else would I place babies on, and beyond, a mountain?'

'But what even is a mountain? And why does it cut off the water?' Then, before she could answer I added, 'And what is beyond?'

'They are all beginnings,' she said, smiling as she squelched.

I scrunched my pretend eyebrows.

'Mysterious ones.'

'No kidding,' I said. I didn't get it.

'Mountains and beyond is a different lore.'

I decided mountains sounded scary. So, I didn't speak or think or move just then.

'Not all mums live by the water, Sprite. Up there is infinite.'

Eel Mother was different. Sorta like she was singing but in a language I couldn't understand. She wasn't colouring either. She was just regular. But glimmering. Everything about this place was unfamiliar. Hard. But kindish, soft at the same time.

'Are there mums on mountains?' I asked.

Eel Mother snuffled, then scooped me up with her tail. She curled her dorsal fin into a perfect little pocket to hold me, then glided in silence through the murky, brownish water.

'So, Eel Mother,' I asked, after a little while, squeezing the question into sweet, light tones. 'How do you work out which mum belongs to what baby? Today was great, by the way.'

'I don't.'

I jerked a bit. 'You don't choose who goes where?'

She scoffed. 'What makes you think I choose?'

I almost fell off her. She was the longest, definitely the oldest, usually the most colourful thing in the water. Plus, now I knew she could fly higher than a mountain. 'Why wouldn't I?'

'I merely deliver.' She stared straight at me, no further explanation offered.

I worked hard to fill the gap. After a short while, I stirred. 'Oh, of course,' I said. 'Great Whale does the choo— the pick—the matching of babies to mother, doesn't he? I get it. You and Great Whale are a team.'

'Not quite,' she added as she swam.

'You aren't togeth—partners, I mean?'

'Of sorts,' she said slowly.

She flashed red in her underbelly. I pretended not to see.

'Well, how's it work?' I urged. 'I definitely deserve to know. Considering all the work I do.' That last part I muttered into my egg so she couldn't hear.

She continued to glide. Eventually she answered. 'Neither I nor Great Whale choose a mother for a birth spirit. Those things are done by ...'

I shuffled a bit, trying to squeeze the answer out of her.

She took in a gulp of water. Slowly she pushed it back through her gills. 'By the air and rain and actions of the day, the cravings and thurstings and tides, the juice and the dry and the way people move. The best way to explain it is ...' She slowed, her movements matching the words that finally spilled from her mouth. 'A mixture of chaos and plan moves babies towards their mums. Always has.' I felt her thick barrel body contract with her breath. I sank into a patch of saggy skin.

'What's that mean?'

'Elements buzzing and surging around each other make the decision. The greatness decides.'

'What about mums who don't want babies, or are bad fisherwomen, or the old girls who don't really like people and just want to do their own thing?'

She shrugged. 'Elements. The greatness.'

'So, a woman who doesn't want babies can still get one?'

'Of course,' was Eel Mother's reply.

'That's not fair!'

Eel Mother laughed.

'But mums who don't want babies ...' I reached for the thought. It was hard. I had no brain or even a skull for it to sit in. 'Well,' I hesitated, 'they will be cranky mothers. And they'll make everyone else cranky too. And that's not good.'

'The greatness,' she repeated. 'All elements, Sprite.'

I felt a bit panicky then. I was worried for all the little spirits that had gone into mums that maybe didn't want them. Maybe cranky people lived on mountains and in the beyond. 'Mums who don't want babies will only end up being their baby's burden.'

She straightened, a warm green speckle flickering up her sides. Eel Mother moved me from her fin to her beak then swished me onto her face. She held my egg sac right below her eye. 'Or their gift,' she said. Moving me to her other eye, she added, 'A baby, though small, is the most powerful thing there is. Able to transform the most stubborn of things.'

Eel Mother obviously didn't understand unborn birth spirit stuff. 'I can't see how.'

'That's because you have no eyes yet.'

We continued to swim. Eel Mother was quiet. I bobbled on her back in silence, watching the strange little flat-nosed fish scan us as we curled past. They hid behind the up-stretched fingers of the mangrove mud, squiggling backwards when we came close. As we continued, Eel Mother swished her tail meat a bit harder and watched all the creatures cower behind their parents to hide amongst the shallows. She also pulsed a red beam and bared her teeth as we cruised. This made shells slam shut and crabs scuttle their babies into their mud-lugged kingdoms. A laugh rippled down her body. 'A little one changes everything, Sprite,' she said as she chuckled to me. 'I think you can see that, even without eyes.'

I wanted to get out of these new waters. They were warmer and murkier and smelled weird. Plus, everything seemed secretive. And scared. I was tired too and put off by Eel Mother and all the stuff she knew and did that I had no clue about. Just before we hit the familiar curve of the outer reaches of the harbour, I asked, 'Can you at least tell me what makes a good mum? So I know and can give her a hand if she needs it.'

'Oh, that doesn't come into it at all,' she said, the spots along her body omitting a green-blue pulse. 'Mums are neither good nor bad at being a mum.'

'Well, how do I know I'll be looked after?' I said, reviving in the saltiness.

'You don't. No one does.'

'That sounds risky to me.'

'As risky as having a baby that doesn't know how to be a good baby.'

Eel Mother laughed. I felt her body jiggle. It bobbled me in my egg sac.

'If a mother knows herself, that's the best that a baby can hope for. Anyway, that's something you don't need to worry about.'

'Yeah, for ages and ages,' I added. I was cranky and tired. My imaginary muscles were sore.

We soon hooked into the current that flowed like a watery curtain to the cave entrance. It had us gliding without effort all the way back to the lair. Eel Mother tipped me from her. I lolloped next to the mound and spread into a blob to stop from rolling around anymore. It had been a big day.

Eel Mother slid next to me, coiling herself around the mound as she always did. She wafted her loose tail over us all. Three sharp pulses, like spasms, coursed through her. I heard clicking tick through her body meat.

'You okay, Eel Mother?'

She pushed a warmish wave over me that melted me back into the salty sea.

I woke to coolness. It startled me. So did the sight of Eel Mother's body stretched outside her lair and beyond the cave entrance.

I slunk as quietly as I could towards her. Hugging a curtain of rock, I saw Great Whale frolicking, trawling his wide barnacled belly over the warm sand of the sheltered cove. I wondered how long they had been sneaking to each other like this.

'Dear Eel Mother,' Great Whale said. 'Join me. Let's rub our backs in the sand together.'

'I have something I wish to discuss.' Eel Mother extended more of herself towards the enormous creature then around his belly in greeting.

'You're troubled.' He righted himself then nuzzled his spout beneath her neck.

'I am.'

'Go on.'

Eel Mother turned towards the sleeping mound.

I darted behind the rock, but I still heard her.

'The clutch is shrinking.'

I peered around the rock to see Eel Mother staring hard into Great Whale's eye.

'Are you sure?' he asked.

'Smaller by the day. Soon there will be no more left to birth.'

Now I looked to the mound. It seemed as high and fat as ever. The spirits were shining their usual sleepy sandy brown.

Great Whale raised his head, his mouth bobbing just below the surface of the water while his enormous bulk scuffed against the sand at the foot of the lair.

'What should I do?' Eel Mother asked.

With deftness and delicacy, Great Whale pushed his mouth fractionally out of the water. He lingered then lowered it, bringing it down again to be completely submerged.

'The great change is upon us, Eel. Creatures unlike those we have seen before are making their way here. They are preparing as we speak.' An ensuing whirlpool from his retracting head created the image. Water monsters with flapping, high wings, carrying ghosts as they scurried upon their backs. I watched the water swirl it into existence, then just as quickly disappear.

'They bring with them waves that will take many away.'

Eel Mother's eyes were wide, her mouth slackened and opened.

'Your clutch shrinks quickly, Eel, because mothers decline. We will lose many, almost all.' Great Whale blinked a tear into the water between them. I watched his sorrow become the water all around.

Eel Mother waved herself closer towards Great Whale. They touched heads. They stayed that way, connected and close, floating in the tides for a long time. It was Great Whale who eventually moved. He lifted a flipper and tenderly placed Eel Mother under it. Then he twisted her, gently, delicately, extracting her from the mound and coiling her around his belly and tail.

'Come,' he said to her. 'Let us enjoy our last dance together.' Eel Mother relaxed into Great Whale's bulk. I told myself not to worry, to remember Eel Mother's promise of a strong, powerful mother waiting for me. As they spun together in the sand, I turned away and wheeled myself back to the mound. It was the right thing to do, to leave them to dance and curl alone.

12.

Eel Mother's head didn't leave the floor for ages after Great Whale's visit. I decided it must be hard when your boyfriend goes away. She went totally floppy and turned a scummy grey. Cause I didn't know about feelings or any of that stuff, I watched her but said nothing. I didn't have the first clue what might make her feel better anyway. I didn't even want her to know I had seen them together.

So, I made myself busy shooing sea lice from her eyes while she breathed. I tickled her tail a bit too, just to make sure she still aerated the spirits. Which she did. But it was more a twitch than a proper fan. Still, all the spirits seemed to get enough turning so that was something, I guess.

Even though I was sad for Eel Mother, I liked the quiet. The galumphing water sounded nice. It was peaceful. Still.

Occasionally Eel Mother opened an eye. When she did, I inched to her to see if she wanted us to start up again. But she usually closed it soon after. And coiled herself away from the opening of her lair. And sucked in slow, watery breaths.

Cause nothing was moving much, all kinds of things started coming closer than they ever had before. Mostly edible-sized creatures like grandad prawns and flighty teen fish. They scoured the overhang wall and ate all the grit and moss and grime they could shovel into their tiny little mouth holes. Most nipped at the greeny thickness then darted away as if their life depended on it. Their nibbles created falling clouds of grime that a carpet of crabs would sideways scuttle to. It was hard not to laugh at them, all tough on the outside but terrified within. I didn't really get why they were so scared. Especially with huge pinching claws that waved in front of them every time they moved.

At one point Eel Mother shifted and the movement caused a line of birth spirits to squirt from the bottom of the mound. They spun towards the overhang. Eel Mother didn't flinch one bit. I took off trying to catch them, but as soon as I did, Eel Mother inhaled. Her jet-suck pulled me from them and back to her. I bumped into her cold folds, and she kept me there with her fin.

The birth spirits tumbled from the edge and into the moss of the overhang wall. Each one lodged amongst the tufts of sea hair that sprouted there. Soon a collection of nibblers, silver biddies and smallish bream mostly came close. They pecked at the moss till each birth spirit had gone whole inside the gullet of a fish. I squirmed to try and save them, but Eel Mother wouldn't loosen her grip on me.

'They'll get there,' she whispered through her nose holes. It was the first time in ages she had spoken. The sound of her voice made my throat juice throb in pain. 'Mums love the taste,' she added. I saw her streak a brighter shade of soggy grey.

'Don't be sad about Great Whale going away.' I nuzzled into her. I made my words flow in time with the current, so they would float out gently, with kindness. 'He'll be back, and you'll be dancing together again soon.'

She tensed. I was worried I had spoiled all the stillness floating between and around us. And given my spying away.

'You have been a wonderful help. And a true gift, Sprite. You know that, don't you?'

I snuggled deeper into her folds. 'And I'm getting stronger I think.' I flexed inside my sac. 'I'm pretty sure I can shove, push and fold even more now. We should get back to work, Eel Mother,' I urged. 'It might help you not be so sad.' My eyes, even though they hadn't arrived, were wide. I still hoped the current was caressing softness into my words.

The cove paused. Fish floated in place, without flicker or movement. All the popping and bobbling and gurgling ceased. It freaked me out. A lot.

'I don't have enough in me, Sprite.' She came in close. 'To get them all born. Things are coming ... I am coming to an end.'

I couldn't talk. Or move. Or think just then.

Eel Mother looked to the mound. 'It's beyond me now.'

She rested her head on the lair floor. I watched as tiny plates of algae flowed in and out of her gills. 'You have to see the rest of the spirits to their mums, my darling, little Sprite.' She closed her eyelids. Her lower jaw dislodged from her beak.

I began buzzing. Fluid churned inside my sac. My insides were swooshing so fast and out of whack with the water it was making me sick. I wanted to tell her that the mound was still huge, that there was work for ages yet. I wanted to convince her she was just sad that Great Whale had left. And she'd feel better about him soon enough, especially if we started up again. But a whiteness had started to spread on her skin. The white of bones and blubber scudding against the sea floor.

I surged towards her and, without mouth or lips, placed a kiss on her beak. The current played amongst her neck rolls. Her jaw wobbled, splayed at an ugly angle from the rest of her crumbling face.

'I don't know how,' I whispered. Or cried. I couldn't tell which.

A crackle pushed from her neck sag. It pulsed through me and then flowed into the cove. It was a slow creak that brought all sorts of swimmy, crawly, scurriey things towards the cave entrance. Sea lice and worms, shellfish of every shine and shape, schools of wrasse and whiting and bream and snapper. Colonies of mulloway and leatherjacket, flathead, garfish, kingfish, parrotfish and cod all arrived. Salmon and mullet joined. A shoal of groupers pulled into ring around all the creatures from the back. Long-armed blue swimmer crabs sidled and snuck between mounds of spanner crabs and Moreton Bays. Wobbegongs glided in, their wide, flat heads resting on the sandbank. The scaled gathering flooded the sea floor.

A pair of eyes spoke first. 'We have come, Old One, as you have asked.'

I watched as the eyes pushed through the surface of the sand to reveal a single, flat sea louse. The creature was a disk with two hairy whiskers that flickered non-stop at the top of its head. Two weird sacs, like mini-mounds, clung to either side of its odd little body. Its tail was a short column that ended in two more tufts of creepy little hairy whisker legs.

Eel Mother blinked her welcome. And thanks.

The mite flicked its tail and the opposite whisker. The sand shimmered again. More eyes pushed up into the sea floor. As far as my unmade eyes could see, the sand was swamped. Covered by every kind and colour of sea lice, mite, sprite, snail, slug and worm.

'Ready, Sprite?' the Boss Louse questioned. Without waiting for a response, he motioned, flicking his antennae in a loud click. The sea floor began moving. Trails of mites and lice, nits and worms formed lines that scaled the overhang wall and entered the lair. They crawled their way past us and to the mound where a single birth spirit was extracted at a time, then handed on their backs down the line. A flurry of larger creatures, crabs and prawns and slugs and such, then ferried them into the waiting mouths of fish. I made my way to the base of the mound as quickly as I could.

The birth spirits were crying as they were plucked and placed and carted away.

'What's going on, Sprite?'

'Are we being kidnapped?'

'They're trying to eat us,' another said, attempting to fall from the back of a broad, orange mite.

'Sprite, go get her. This doesn't feel right,' cried one.

'I'm scared!'

'Yes, please, please, Sprite. Get Eel Mother. We'll all be eaten if you don't.'

'Eel Mother … has asked them …' I spluttered. It was difficult to talk with so many hard things all happening at once. 'Her friends will take you into a mum.'

The spirits wailed, a chorus of worry weaving amongst the currents. Their tiny voices pleaded. 'We don't want to go with them!'

'They're scary. We want you.'

'And Eel Mother. Their teeth are sharp.'

'And their eyes move weird,' a tiny one squeaked.

I scanned the line. A heap of birth spirits were being placed into the mouth of a Kingfish, its yellow tail wafting as both its eyes darted independently of each other.

'Where is she?' came the yell from a spirit. 'Where is Eel Mother? We need her, Sprite.'

I made myself as big as I could.

'Friends,' I started loudly, pretending I was calm. 'You are beginning your great adventure into going into a mum. Eel Mother has asked me to take charge. She is … resting. She's tired.' I tried hard to keep my voice straight and not wavy or sad. 'She's asked me to take charge of you.' I snuck a sideways glance at her. Her eyes were dull and still. 'I have been watching the wonderful ways she has birthed you all and I have learned so much from her. I know how to get you safely to a mum. All these creatures of the harbour, our neighbours and family, will see you to mothers who are waiting for you in the above.'

The line paused. Shafts of light glinted in the cove.

'About time you earned your keep,' a cheeky spirit sang. Movement returned, the line shaking with energy and effort. 'Maybe we'll meet in the above, Sprite. I'll give you a good, hard whack on the shoulders as thanks if we do.'

I felt good just then. And big. Strong. So, I kept at it. Shouting encouragement to the procession of passing spirits.

'Don't forget to chew your food when you get teeth and feel everything when you get hands and can pick up stuff,' I said.

'And smell the air,' one added.

'And jump so high your foot bones shake,' another added.

'That's right, friends. Do all those things. And do them well. With everything that you are,' I shouted.

'Thanks, Sprite, for reminding us,' one said as it twirled past, handed on by the mites.

'You'll know so much soon when you're all born. I'm happy for you. I truly am!' I yelled down the line.

The creatures at the end of the line were loaded up then zoomed off in all directions, into the harbour. It all happened fast after that. I watched a crab, balancing pools of birth spirits, sand scuttle then disappear in a fluff along the ocean floor.

In no time at all, the mound vanished.

The birth spirits had been deposited to all parts of the harbour to go into their mums. Only Eel Mother and I remained in the lair.

As darkness covered the cove and soft silver flakes rested on the water, I moved close to dear Eel Mother. I could tell she was smiling, despite how she looked – all broken down and collapsing. I knew if she could have spoken, she would have said I did well. And probably that she loved me too. I snuggled into her and gazed into the shimmering silver pools that wobbled on the water. The lair and the cove slowed. My insides did too. With no one left but me and a fading Eel Mother, all I could do was sync with the sea.

13.

Kill Ya Darlings

Ginny surveyed her desk and the small pink shredder before her. After all the office shredder crap she'd come across — researching run times, bin volumes, cut types and security levels — she had ended up googling Kmart ones instead. She was scrolling deep, well into looking at lower end options, when she'd seen it. In the children's craft section. Pink. And only three bucks. By some happy coincidence, she realised its feeder was the exact same width as the pages of her notebooks. It was one of the few details Ginny had forgot to check in her extensive research. But the match of paper to feeder width meant the shredding process would be quick. And this was a good thing. Exactly what she needed.

If she had time to reread entries before they were minced, she might think twice about destroying them. And the memories they contained. But now, with this pretty, cheap little beauty, all that was required was a tear from the guts and the cranks of a retractable plastic handle.

The notebook stack, mostly a vomit of cheap Kmart and Woollies diaries, was a hefty presence on her desk. It was a shame job, looking at them piled up.

'The sooner I shift this, the better,' she said.

Filling her chest with a fortifying breath, Ginny committed to a linear progression. The earliest entries, messy biro scribblings on thin, coffee-stained pages, would need to be the first to go.

She cringed as she sorted them. Each journal trumpeted a tired motivational quote – *The Best Things are Not Things*, *You Got This*, and *Dream Big* stared, doe-eyed at their executioner from the desk. The only notebook she now considered vaguely acceptable was a hardcover banksia and cockatoo print. She picked it up.

'Yuck,' she said, scanning the pages, the inky swirls reacquainting Ginny with earlier versions of herself. 'At least it'll make a shit-tonne of paper.' Ginny slammed the notebook shut. She scoffed as she read the inscription on its back cover, *Designed and Printed in China*.

'Consider yourself repatriated.' She straightened, pulling her shoulders back and down. 'And congratulations on joining the Dreamtime Books family. Welcome, welcome, welcome.'

Ginny scooped up a lined A5 Woolworths special. Flicking open the pink plastic cover, she grasped a handful of pages. They tore easily away from the coated, metallic binding. Clutching a wad, she put them into the protected teeth of the shredder and cranked. The thin pieces sliced like butter, coiling into ribboned strips in the compact, plastic tray. She ripped again and repeated. Blade slicing through paper delighted her. It was seamless – measured and precise. As she continued to feed and slash, Ginny noted, with some mirth, that her words became most sturdy in the moment they were ribboned to smithereens.

Again, she tore and cranked, this time catching the hint of a stanza. Some foolishness about wanting and temptation. *If you were the type that held hands/I think I might/Explode/Then die/Happily/Clasped/By you.*

'Publishing's a tough business,' she said, relishing the smoothness of the carve that dismembered her old words and stale self. 'Kill ya darlings and all that.'

Pleased, she took in the clear plastic tub beneath the mechanism. Breathing deeply, she stared into the tray. Ginny could just read a cleaved line, thinned but still intact. The sliced pages had, for the most part, transformed her diary into bleached alphabet spaghetti. All except this one line. It was a direct quote from Nath. She remembered the exact moment he'd said it. What he was wearing. The precise angle of the sun. She read the words aloud. They arrived mostly as breath. 'It is what it is.'

Ginny lifted the lid from the toy-turned-machine and removed the strands. She jammed the shredded reams into a calico library bag she had rescued from the gutter grid at the entrance to the local primary school. Then she pulled its rope, stringing it shut. She placed the swelling bump on her writing table next to her pile of condemned notebooks.

She leaned towards the stack. 'You're going to a better place,' she whispered. The stilled, sliced sacrifice weighed down the room. To release its weight, she added, 'Trust me, I'm a CEO.'

When the last of the Woolworths A5 had twisted into the bottom of the catcher, Ginny shoved the curled reams into the calico pouch. She let her hand run through the spirals. The streams sizzled as she swished them. The most intimate parts of her life were now dismembered and crammed into some kid's lost library bag. She ran her hands through them, caressing the past, grasping the future.

14.

From then on, all I did was watch Eel Mother. Like a hungry shark. Her skin was fading, getting whiter and hollower with each turn of tide. It was lucky she was so bulky. If she wasn't, she most likely would have been sucked out of the cave and been rubbed away by the sea floor till there was none of her left.

After watching more and more fish come and nip at the moss growing at the overhang entrance, I wondered if Eel Mother might be hungry too. So, I covered myself in the sludge and rubbed my sac all over her raggedy teeth pillars and beak and stuff. I didn't know if it would help her. But it sort of felt like the right thing to do.

Her face relaxed and went floppy a bit. That helped me squeeze into her hard-to-get cheek and beak parts. And cause her jaw was all out of whack, I left a pile of slimy stuff in a dip near her throat. She stayed still and blinked.

Once I thought she smiled but it was more a sad collapse than any kind of happy, broken-mouth stretch.

Watching Eel Mother flop around in the swell made me panic a bit, like an ice-cold blast of current overtook me and shivered me out of my own self.

To keep myself from worrying, I started really listening to the sounds of the cove. At first it was the hardest thing I had ever done. Everything was bubbly. Like a water blur. But soon I could hear all sorts of taps and crackles and beats. There was always creaking or moaning or humming going on. When I tried copying the rhythms, they would come back at me, louder and a bit questiony, like I was in a conversation but didn't know the language.

I started repeating the noises back to the harbour. I hoped I was saying nice or clever things. I'd always send the sound off with a kind thought, so if my sea language was wrong, the feeling would make up for it. It's something I thought Eel Mother would like me to do. I'd send her regards too. That always brought back a pretty call or an extra sharp snap or creak. Sometimes, when it went a bit quiet, I would send smiles into the warm water streaks that flowed past the inlet. Or things I imagined smiles to be anyway.

As for the spirits, most had been born and were probably grown up by now. Maybe even their babies were spirits in the mound now. I sent good thoughts and happy wishes to them, whatever they were doing. I thought about telling them that Eel Mother was unwell, but I didn't want them to worry so I didn't put that in.

I took to giving Eel Mother reports on what I heard and who I sent respects and good thoughts to. She liked it, I think. Although she was whiter and wrinklier than ever, she would sometimes send tiny flicks of colour to a handful of squiggles at her beak when she heard something she liked. So I kept doing it.

I cried once when she flickered in time with a story. I was telling her of a passing giant squid. The blue on her beak was a sorry, mournful shade. It held nothing like her regular shine. I knew it was the only way she could speak to me then. And I loved her harder than ever for it, although her love was fading and dim and about to finish up for good probably.

When all the clacking and clicking and stories had been shared, there was nothing left to do besides join with the rhythms of Eel Mother's slowing. I became motionless like her. Although I had never taken a breath, I laboured to breathe. My heart, which of course hadn't even arrived inside a chest yet, slowed. I was heavy and draggy and low. Death seemed peaceful. Like a flowing out wave or receding tide. With a final push of effort, I lodged myself under a billow of Eel Mother's belly flop. It wasn't as heavy as I remembered. I squelched in there and was pretty snug, all dark and draped in dying skin. So, when he arrived, it took me by complete surprise.

I only realised he was there cause his eye swallowed the entire lair entrance and blocked out everything else. That and the ringing voice coming from his great humped body that shook the walls of the cave. It was so full it shuddered me out of my together dying.

'Sister,' came the echoey address. 'I am come to see you.'

I wasn't sure if it was right for me to look at Great Whale. I pushed myself deeper into Eel Mother's folds. I was surprised to notice her breath and beat and warmth meet me.

I felt her body tightening. And saw pulses of colour returning. Soon faded yellows and reds and greens were making waves upon the folds of her weakened skin. I was so happy I did a front twirl inside my sac. Then I spun backwards, in a matching reverse one. It was wonderful to see Eel Mother revive. I didn't care that it was for a sweetheart and not me.

Her bulk shifted and started to rise. I moved with her, still lodged in her folds. Fresh water gushed over me. The newness of the flow made my sac sizzle. Soon, a cloudy, smoky, dirt grey Eel Mother snaked us out of the cave and towards the Whale now bobbing in the cove.

I think they kissed. Or maybe spoke or touched heads or something. I didn't think it polite to watch. Quickly, I found myself being pulled towards their heads. I did a little squeal. I had forgotten how much I loved being bossed and pushed and drawn in by my beautiful Eel Mother. She bent her nose so that I skidded along her beak and into my favourite wrinkle just above it. She balanced me there, the way it used to be.

Great Whale came close, his fullness blocking out the rest of the harbour. Bracketed curves of blubber framed his eye so that there seemed nothing else existing in the world. It also made him look pretty smart, like his face was crunched in thought all the time. His black eye stared straight into me.

I waited for him to speak.

He just stared.

So, I thought maybe he wanted me to say something. Just as I was about to, he turned his enormous self away.

'Such … simplicity,' he said, curling himself into a beam of warmer water.

I watched as his tail, now dangling in front of us, blocked out the harbour. Eel Mother wobbled, feebly snaking onto Great Whale's back blubber. He rose himself to meet her. Taking her weight with a flap of his tail, we thrust forward at once. I was spun backwards in the wrinkle by Great Whale's surge. Eel Mother rippled purple streaks a fair way down her body. I watched gold flecks try to ignite between the streaks. It was as if she was rocketing through the water the way she used to, sending beaming colours into every corner of the harbour again.

I stayed in her wrinkle, really hoping Eel Mother would ignite. But I tried not to watch too closely. Her moments were precious and she was delicate. And together they had a way of acting like they were the only ones in the sea. So, I concentrated on the bubbles made by Great Whale's tail swirls. They churned and fizzed everything around.

A gang of leatherjackets were catapulted into endless backflips. I ducked into the wrinkle when we zoomed past them so I could let out my enormous inside laugh. I don't really like leatherjackets too much. They're usually mean and like picking on smaller things.

Creatures began gathering in the bubbles, trailing behind us as we swam. Most of them had their mouths open. I can understand why. In our little part of the harbour, it wasn't often you saw really big fish. And Great Whale was a really, really, really big fish. He was so old his barnacles had an oyster beard that hung from his chin. They swished as he moved and made their very own slipstream. It kind of dawned on me how lucky I was just then. Even though no one could see me, I was known by some pretty large boss fish. I had some wonderful, powerful connections.

15.
A Personal Question

Ginny never rummaged through other people's household throw-outs. There was no need. Things she needed just made their way to her. All her doilies, hand-embroidered, came from under the bench at the bus stop. She found her bedside lamp, with working bulb, in the alleyway. If she ever needed anything specific, she always picked it up at Vinnies. Salvos if she was desperate. All the stuff there had been vetted. And cleaned. By fussy old white women who were still about standards.

When the busted tallboy appeared in front of the unit four doors down, she knew her neighbours, the Tie-Dyes, were moving. And they for sure would have a garage sale. They'd think it cool. And they probably needed the cash. If the state of the tallboy was anything to go by.

Their clear-out happened in a series of episodes. She clocked it each morning, as she returned from her early morning coffee and diary session. The flimsy, metal drying rack that went out on Tuesday was joined by a bread bin on Thursday. The *For Lease* sign went up a day later. *Don't fancy trying to find a place now, poor buggers*, she thought. *But there's two of them. They'll be right.*

Ginny had seen the tenants of the flat only twice before, both times they were sitting on their front step, drinking wine from glass jars in the afternoon sun. She called them The Tie-Dyes because of the huge square of patterned, coloured fabric slung across their front window. Today, a plastic table of overflowing bric-a-brac, knick-knacks and miscellaneous tidbits were laid out for all the street to see. And rummage through. And pick over. She saw it clearly from halfway along the street. The nature strip narrowed thanks to cardboard boxes filled with pots and appliances that spilled from the table's underbelly.

She shot the dude a quick smile. One of those *just passing through* ones. He nodded as she swept past.

His housemate, a scraggly, light brunette in a three-quarter tank top, called to her. 'Hey,' she said, eyes widening as Ginny approached.

Ginny smiled and tilted her neck, making sure her headphones glinted in a ray of early sun.

'You're the girl down the back, aren't you?'

Ginny extracted a bud from her ear. 'Moving?' she said, pointing at a tarnished candelabra.

'Oh yeah,' said the girl. 'Rent's gone up, can't do it anymore. I'm Steph,' she said, offering her hand.

Ginny shook it.

'That's Robbo.' She pointed.

'G'day,' said the bloke plonking a stagnant green gloop lava lamp on his end of the table.

'Ginny. When are you out?'

'Wednesday,' said Steph. 'Thought we'd see if we could shift some crap instead of pack it.'

'Yeah,' scoffed Robbo. 'Might make enough for a couple of satay sticks.'

'Where are you going?' Ginny asked, scanning the utensils. She noticed a sparkling fairy figurine next to a tired, plastic spatula. She picked it up and held it in her palm.

'Dollar fifty,' said Steph. 'Birthday present from an ex. Can you believe? What a weirdo.'

'Poor old Twaddle Dick.' Robbo laughed, fussing over his display.

Steph rolled her eyes. 'Robbo's taking off to Cairns, bastard. I'll go bunk with my sister in Canberra for a while.'

Ginny placed the fairy between a soup ladle and a corkscrew.

'We used to try and guess what your job was,' Steph said, nodding at Robbo. 'He thought you were a nurse. I reckon you work at a day care or something. You look kind.'

Ginny snorted. 'Or tired.'

'And you're quiet as the proverbial,' chimed Robbo, dusting a black gaming keyboard with the edge of his sleeve. 'Don't reckon we've heard a squeak from you in the three years we've been here.'

'That long, geeze.'

'One stage I thought maybe you worked … the night, if ya know what I mean? Was only a theory though. No proof,' he said, eyes wide.

'Jesus you're a knob,' Steph shot back.

'So, what is it you do?' Robbo said, picking up a red bar towel, and after sniffing it, chucking it at Steph's head.

'I work in publishing,' Ginny said.

Robbo straightened. 'Ya know Stephen King?' he said, picking up a ragged paperback and waggling it towards Ginny. The embossed metallic letters of its title glinted in the sun. 'Six bucks. For a masterpiece. And pass on my regards to old Kingy – when you see him next. What a lege!'

'Can I ask a personal question?' Steph said, her voice lowering as she leaned in.

Ginny noticed the back of Steph's hair. Its tangled mess still held a pillow's imprint.

'How can you afford to live here?' Not waiting, she continued. 'I know it's a studio, laundry in the kitchen probably, but you live by yourself. That guy used to visit but ...' Steph trailed off. 'I only ask because we can barely afford the rent and we both work two jobs.'

Ginny noticed how blue Steph's eyes were. The same colour twinkled from the glitter in the fairy's skirt. Twaddle Dick was a romantic.

'Community housing,' she said.

'That flat's a houso?' burst Robbo.

'Shut up, dickhead,' Steph yelled back.

Ginny stared, trying to suss if Robbo was full crouching hipster hidden racist or just some loose dude who never thought before he spoke and didn't ever expect he needed to. In short, a man.

'Aboriginal Community Housing.' She kept her eyes on him.

'Knew it,' he said, turning to Steph. 'Told ya, didn't I?'

'I'm sorry,' she replied. 'He's not right in the head. Or mouth,' she added through pursed lips.

'What?' he said, palms lifted. 'I didn't say anything offensive. Did I?' he asked, shuffling closer towards the pair. 'It's subsidised. So what? The least they deserve. We voted yes, didn't we, Steph?' he said, turning to Ginny and waggling a finger at his fellow tie-dye housemate. 'And most of our mates did too, I'm pretty sure.'

'Jesus, Robbo, will you just—'

'The whole thing was a fair-dinkum shit show, not helped by some of your lot, if I'm honest. But we were eighty-six per cent yes in this booth. I checked. Must count for something.'

Ginny stared at a faded oven mitt towards Steph's end of the table. Its yellow background a caricature of an Aboriginal warrior standing on one leg, balancing himself with a spear. *Ayers Rock* was printed in seventies bubble font below the man, the red rock dominating the background horizon.

'Family holiday. Years back,' Steph blurted. She swiped the mitt off the table and threw it into a box underneath.

'I went there too,' added Robbo. 'Aussie Rules tour, couple of years ago. Sacred place. Not like this overpriced shit hole.'

Ginny moved to Robbo's end of the table. A pile of stickers were flayed in a farewell fan. Yellow letters dissected the black and red background: *You are on Gadigal Land*. Ginny knew these were produced by the office of the local Greens member. Free for anyone who asked. She picked them up.

'Five bucks, the lot.'

Staring directly at Robbo, Ginny dropped the stickers into her bag. Then, digging her AirPods into her ears again, she turned from them and walked off.

Returning from the library later that evening, Ginny found a blender placed in the middle of her front step. A yellow post-it note read, *Brand new, hope it can be of use, Steph xxx*.

16.

The three of us glided into a bay. The water, shallow and crisp, sparkled shards of lime green against the bleached yellow sandbank below. Eel Mother, cradled against Great Whale's back, tried to flicker colours but nothing could penetrate the bright white of her skin. With his fin, Great Whale scooped aside a patch of sand and made a depression. He tilted, and Eel Mother tumbled from his back, floating to the beach floor like a ribbon of lost seaweed. I fell with her.

When we hit the seabed, I fell from her back and bobbled under his oystery beard. I checked to see if Eel Mother was okay. All I could see was the whale shaping a delicate wall of sand around her. His flipper was wide and flat, but he moved it with tenderness and incredible care. After he had encased Eel Mother in her sand bed, her limp body stopped its all-over-the-place rocking. I turned cool, sadness blooming out of me as I realised Eel Mother now needed to be protected from the sea after commanding it for so long. Nestled in the shallow grave, she appeared whiter than ever, the colours of life almost gone.

'Would you like some food, Eel Mother?' I called to her. 'Maybe I can get you some?' I scanned the inlet for some rocks or moss or something, but it was too clean. Clear. Then Eel Mother lifted her out-of-whack head to speak to Great Whale who was watching, floating above her. As she did, a razor-sharp tooth fell from her mouth.

My throat part seized. My eye spaces stung.

I rushed towards her and forced myself over the top of the sand wall. I could see Great Whale's shadow moving with me. A gigantic flat flipper covered with barnacles wafted above me. Before he could scoop me away from her side, Eel Mother lifted her tail, caressing Great Whale. She placed it across his flubbery flipper and stopped its movement. They bobbled there, holding hands like that right above my head part.

'It's time,' he said.

Eel Mother nuzzled her broken face into me. A crunch of sand dug beneath it and lifted me. Her eyeball had glowy, shiny things that twinkled in the darkness of her pupil. The speckles were new. They were deep. And went for ages. Way back and never-ending inside her eye channel.

Because I knew her so well and loved her lots, I could hear her speak, even though her mouth was all wrong and didn't work anymore.

'She's here, Sprite.' Eel Mother shifted. The movement must have hurt her. I watched a wincing ripple flash down her spine.

A wave of heat shot through me. Then a jet of freezing flowed in. I started to buzz. I began to fidget.

'She's ready,' Eel Mother told me in her thinking speech.

I fizzed a bit. It made my imaginary breath short and my insides a mushy swirl. I worried that Eel Mother may not be strong enough to spit or chuck or hurl me into my mum. I worried I wouldn't know what to do when I was in her. Would she even know about me being there? Would I grow all the bits I needed in the right ways and turn out to be a good baby that was kind and didn't cry and demand things all the time? I didn't even know if I knew how to speak the right language to a mum.

'Eel Mother,' I said, folding myself into her puckering white side. 'I need to stay with you a bit longer.'

Before she could respond, oars dug into the water's surface. A slender shadow brought a gliding canoe over the top of us and into the shallows. An army of mites rose from the beach floor to spit and shovel sand around the bark bottom, keeping it secure and holding it in place. More scampered and scurried all over the canoe's hull, cleaning and stripping it by nibbling the algae and sea scum from its belly and sides. We watched as a pair of delicate feet stepped into the water and scuffed the sand. Grains rose then settled around the toes. The ankles were elegant. Thin. Peering closer, I saw marks, pools of missing skin spotted around the ankles and up the slender calves. It was weird because I had only just seen them, but I loved everything about those feet and legs and ankles and hairs and mysterious missing bits just then.

I came out closer for a better look. As I did, another pair of feet joined, walking into the quiet waves from the shore. These new feet were flat and broad. There were sprouts of wiry hair springing out of the toes and the top of the foot. They looked like curls of kelp, just not as wide and rubbery. The same kind of growth shot up the leg and probably continued into the above. Maybe. It was the first time I had seen feet so I really couldn't be sure.

The two sets of feet came closer until they almost touched. I watched the toes dig a little into the sand. It was sort of weird then because, although we were in the water, everything seemed still. All of the swaying was going on in the above. Then, just like that, the smaller, slighter feet disappeared. They rose from the water and were gone. Only the wider, hairier ones remained, pushed deeper, sitting further into the sand.

'Where did she go?' I blurted, a ripple pushing out of my jerky start.

Out of nowhere, a hot pain entered my middle. I got panicky. A slow, sliding moan echoed throughout the cove. Eel Mother rose, belly up, her dislodged jaw hanging at a sickening angle in the still water. All I could do was watch her piercing whiteness drift from me and towards the crying whale that lurked low in the shallows. It was then that the single pair of hairy feet waded through the wash and disappeared back into the above.

Eel Mother was gone. Great Whale was heartbroken. My mum had arrived then disappeared. And I had missed it all, and, with it, my only chance of ever being born.

17.

I bobbled in the shallows. For how long I didn't know. Nothing mattered then cause I had been left alone. I was furtherest away from being born than a thing that lived and breathed and laughed in the above had ever been. I decided it best to just scrape myself into the bottom of the harbour. Let my sac scuff up and become forgotten grains of sand or something.

I drifted. Without care or wish of what to be.

I skimmed against mites' whiskers. They seemed to have hairy little barbs. They tickled and stabbed at my shell. I heard chittering too. They were probably laughing at me, rolling aimlessly in the shallows. A blob of nothingness. Alone. Forlorn. But I didn't care about anything then. There was no point anymore.

The shallow waters I scudded against began to warm. It got hot. I could feel the above throb into my shell. I thought that I might boil and maybe that was the way I would end. I'd bubble into birth spirit juice and then sizzle into steam. I tried to relax my insides and wait for nothingness.

The grains on the beach floor were really yellow. Somehow they changed into a weird brownish shade. It may have been interesting once. It was just a happening now, a shift that had no meaning. To a nothing like me. I gazed, not caring, at the grains. The longer I did, the more colours arrived. Pink and orange and mauve then no colour, see-through specks. Loose layers pitched in the brightness. They tried to dance, to get me to care, jostling and moving together in the invisible current.

I laughed at myself then, knowing I had realised too late the detail of what surrounded me. I was annoyed I was seeing things and learning stuff when there was no reason to know anymore. The beach clicked and muffled as I drifted amongst the grains. A flurry of movement brought with it a distant hiss. I pushed backwards then upside down to look. A wave of mites sped towards me. They surged over each other, hurling themselves off the crest of the wave their bodies created. Jumping and hurtling and cannoning over themselves, the mites swept me up and carried me towards the far end of the beach. I thought I could hear them. Squeals and giggles mostly. At least they were having a good time. Their laughter made me retract myself into my silent middle. If I had had a belly button, I would have been holed up there, sulking.

The mite wave gathered pace. It whooshed me into cooler, bright waters. There, a small depression created a deeper spot, an underwater pool at the end of the beach. A handful of whiting speared out of the way as the mites pushed me towards it.

'Ready, Sprite?' a lice yelled before being swallowed by the cascading horde.

'Too bad if you're not.'

'I think I can see her,' one squealed as it fell.

'Just as Eel Mother said she would be,' shouted another.

My chest part twinged from hearing Eel Mother's name, but the feeling was knocked out of me as I whacked into a partly submerged head. It slammed me into the round of my sac.

The mites secured me into a heap of tangled black curls. Then they dispersed. I struggled amongst the new messiness. I rose with the hair as the body lifted out of the water and pushed into the strong, sharp brightness of the above.

When we began moving, I gasped, unsure if I would be able to breathe air. But the hair coiled around me and pooled bubbles of saltwater for me to suck on. Hanging tight, I could see the ends of the swaying locks beneath me. But being in the above and in air mucked me up. I felt like I had weight pressing down, wanting to squish me into juice or something. It didn't hurt. But it didn't feel nice either.

As the body moved, I tried to lean into the heaviness. Pretending the swaying was the water's current helped a bit. I decided I'd try to make friends with the weight, let it decide what was best. Through a peep hole between the curls, I saw a beach from above for the very first time. The sand was almost white where the young sun hit it. The water of the shoals was a crying crystal green. The sand scutted away from the harbour to a line of uneven, collapsing stone boulders – bigger than any underwater ones I had seen before. They looked pretty much like mega grains of beach sand. Shrubs scrambled over the further away ones, while fat, darker trees overtook a hill behind. A white mist hung around the tips of the leaves. I made out a hint of little yellow fruit, dotted amongst the dark green, hanging from spiralling branches. Most of the treetops were covered in a blanket of fog.

A rising plume of smoke spiralled from the sand. A glowing orange crackle bubbled at its base.

Movement suddenly ceased. Hair rose like a shock from the scalp beneath me. My top part tingled. That's probably when I first felt how my own head would be. Through strands of hair I watched a figure approach. I recognised the broad, hairy feet straight away. A man walked from the darkness and strode into a shaft of sunlight. The skin beneath me got all tight. Then hard. Heat prickled across the scalp as the man came closer. I was pretty sure then I was on top of a mum. But I couldn't work out who the man was though. Or why he'd be there when I was about to go in.

Body lines pulsated beneath Mum's skin and all her rhythms quickened. Her breath became shallow and fast. The man came close then touched Mum's arm. Driving waves of heat, full and hungry, pulsed up and down her head, her skin and in her hair. A hand came into the strands. I dodged the fingers as it ruffled around. A shiver came into her body. It rippled through me as well. It took her back down, into the shallows. I tingled as Mum floated beside the man in the shallows of the breaking crystal water.

I exploded with the movements igniting beneath me. Waves pushed onto the sand. Tides rushed into the rip. Grains shifted and were shoved around the above. Blood pumped. Bodies rolled. Hands grabbed. Skin and hair and faces pushed. In all the whirring, I lost my grip and fell from hair onto face. I cried out for help cause I was scared of all the movement and weight of where I was. The mites were the only things I could think to call out to. I worried I would fall back into the water. Become a lonely nothing again.

Instead, I was swallowed by a bead of sweat. It trickled me from a forehead onto the tip of a nose. My mum threw back her head. This thrust me onto the edge of her lip. I teetered, wobbling in my new fresh-salty form. Her tongue came out. She licked me.

I tried to call to Eel Mother. To rouse on her for not saying goodbye and to thank her for all she had shown and taught and made me do. For being my friend, a teacher, and the only one I ever knew or needed. But I was swallowed. My short time in the above ended with me travelling into the pit of a woman, through the sweat she made and shared with the man.

She stood soon after. I knew cause I could feel her moving. Somehow I could also see with her eyes. Standing in the shallows, the man joined her. She leaned into him, their fast-beating bodies relaxing, becoming one. Mum raised her hand to shield her eyes from the sun's glare. The man's hand came up and rested on her shoulder. Not far from shore, a barnacle-laden fin slapped the water's surface. It sent spray into the air. After another blow the fin disappeared and the water stilled. Mum melted into the man's chest. Behind us, on the shore, leaves and bark rattled as a creature, a lizard or mouse maybe, hurried through the leafy undergrowth. Then a great roar and fizz saw the elongated underside of a surging Great Whale push through the surface and soar into the above. His magnificence rotated with the momentum of the rise. His white belly turned and presented his deep blue head. The man raised an open palm to the surging creature. Mum bent forward and scooped a handful of wet sand into her mouth. I scanned Great Whale's bulk. As he curled from us and began to descend, Great Whale found me, tucked inside my mum. His eye locked on mine – or the place I imagined my eyes to be. Holding my gaze, he showed me Eel Mother, now glowing and glinting every kind of colour that had ever existed, her own wondrous beauty farewelling me from her new home within his eye.

Mum spat the wet sand into the shallows. Its splatter matched the spray of Great Whale's return to the water. The man stroked Mum's hair. Together they smiled, then walked arm in arm back to their fire on the warming, waking sand.

Part Two

the round

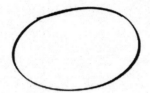

18.

Red Gum and Turpentine

Ginny had walked past the nursery heaps of times before, but never entered. She was a plant snob. She didn't own any because she didn't think much of potted flowers. They weren't the real deal.

They don't have street smarts, she thought as she stepped into the shop's dank cool. And street smarts were what got her to this point. And was exactly what Dreamtime Books was looking for.

Ginny meandered along the narrow walkways lined by sturdy, deep green foliage and made her way to what she assumed was the shop's back wall. Here multicoloured glass birds were welded to metal frames. A selection of orange and yellow mandala stickers and fake dreamcatchers hovered from ceiling beams in their nylon line suspenders. Clunky cylindrical wind chimes drooped lifeless against the corrugated tin interior. Walking closer, her toe scuffed the hoof of a metallic deer. A pair of gawky flamingos ogled her as she checked the ground for damage.

Gammon, she thought. *Nothing in here makes sense.*

She edged closer to a display rack of hand-held tools and garden utensils. Ginny reached for a pair of gloves, one side green non-slip rubber, the other illustrated with white flannel flowers. She looked at the price tag. 'A hundred and fifteen bucks?' she barked. In the recoil of her head, she caught the glimpse of a pink-cheeked garden gnome. It stared at her from its shelf, a half-baked smirk rising from its bushy white moustache. 'Argh,' she shivered, returning the gloves.

'Can I help you, at all?' came a voice from behind. A slim man in tight, khaki King Gees slid behind her.

Ginny turned to face him 'Nah, I'm—'

'Is there anything particular you're looking for?'

She pointed to the packets of seeds in the display ahead.

'Ooh yes, we've had some new Murnong Yam Daisy seedlings just come in,' King Gee said, reaching past the seed packets and picking up a plant. 'And we also have some new Finger Limes in stock. And I think—', he added, bending again. 'Yes, here it is,' he said, placing down the first plant and picking up another. 'We have one Rosella left. Isn't she a beauty?' He twirled the pot around to reveal a single pursed red bud. 'They really are wonderful,' he added, gazing at the plant. 'You must be really pleased.'

'Pardon?'

'With,' he shrugged, 'these.' He held the pot up to her.

'They're great,' she said slowly, searching for a waft of clarity. 'I guess.' *Maybe those shorts have cut off circulation to this brain,* she thought.

'They're one of a kind. Especially rare around here these days,' King Gee continued. 'We get all our natives from you. It's a pleasure to support community. Of course, we understand it's hard to keep up with demand but we're fine to take it as slow as you need. Hopefully you'll be able to fill our order soon. But ... the seasonal conversation is a great one too.'

Ginny frowned and shook her head.

'Black Fingers,' he replied.

Ginny cackled. 'I'm sorry, what?'

'The bush tucker nursery,' King Gee said. 'Based at Lapper Ruse? Black Fingers,' he said with emphasis, concisely.

'From where?' she asked, her nose scrunching and forehead rippling into deep lines.

'Here,' he said, pulling a phone from his back pocket and bringing the website up on his screen.

'Oh, La Pa,' Ginny stated, biting hard on her lip. 'I thought you said—'

'Black Fingers, a First Nations enterprise – working on homelands, beautiful Bidjigal Country. See?' he read. He placed the pot on the floor and ran his fingers through his fringe.

'Yeah, that looks great,' she said, gathering her composure. 'But I just came in for some seeds. Angophora and Turpentine to be precise.'

'You're not from Black Fingers Nursery?'

She shook her head.

The man straightened. 'I didn't mean t—we don't get man—'

Ginny cocked her head and raised her eyebrows, daring him to continue.

He cleared his throat. 'Those are some substantial plants. Huge root systems. Sounds like you've got big plans?'

Ginny scoffed. 'Not Black Fingers big,' she said, 'but yeah, I have plans.'

'And you've calculated the space needed for these trees?'

'Yep.'

'Because there aren't many places left around here that could support their growth successfully.'

'I know a few.'

'Really? Where?'

Ginny stared him down. She could feel every plastic and metal and plaster eye from every creepy creature in his shop join the face-off.

'Not at liberty,' she replied straightening. 'Culturally sensitive info at the moment.' Then, spotting the paper packet hanging on the wall, she lurched forward. 'Ah ha!' she said reaching past him and grabbing it. 'And here!' She grabbed a second bag. 'Perfect.' After a quick side-eye, she added, 'Register this way?' Ginny began walking towards where she assumed the service desk would be. King Gee followed and rung up the packets of seeds.

'Six dollars fifty,' he said. 'And check with your local—'

'The Old People will be really pleased with these,' she said, pushing out a fake smile, interrupting his council-planting-regulation sermon. She tapped her phone on the payment terminal and walked towards the exit. Before she left the shop's cool shade, she read the sign above the door: *A beautiful oasis in an ugly city.*

'The ugliest things are your gnomes, mate,' Ginny muttered, stepping into the blaring sunlight. She crossed the road and walked down the hill towards her home, planning the steps she would need for her first batch of Dreamtime Books paper. Its very first run would be soaked, sifted and pressed from the ruins of her life, and grow into the city's newest patches of remnant forest – Red Gum and Turpentine sprouting from her words.

19.

Mum's cave was round. And small. And full of warm wetness. That much I could tell even upside down and halfway in. I knew, before all of me plopped inside, it would be syrupy. And yucky gluggy. I screwed up my lip bit then felt a buzz in what was probably going to be a cheek or nose.

It was weird having parts talk to each other, even though they weren't there yet. Spose they knew they would all be face family one day. These twitches made a bit more of me squiggle down through Mum's belly. With my added weight, I began to droop from the roof of her cave.

I wondered if I should try to breathe. I sort of felt I should. So, I took in a suck and let the warmth flow into me. I whirlpooled inside myself. I took another gulp. Again, another inside swirl. It didn't feel that terrible. After a few more swiggy swallows, I got used to the idea of taking stuff in and having it smooch around inside me. To tell the truth, if I had thought about dripping upside down through a belly gland and having to suck sweet mum cave water, I might not have wanted to come. But maybe that's what happens when the thing you hope and wish and dream for finally comes true. It felt scary and confusing and wonderful all at the same time.

From what I could make out, the lining of her insides were pink. But the more I looked at it, the more it changed. Within belly ruffles it was red. On surfacy bits it seemed orange. I decided belly cave pink but sometimes red with orange blushes was going to be my favouritest colour of all time.

The skin of Mum's cave was all curves and creases. They billowed everywhere in a big round curtain. From the top of the cave, I could see some folds were fat enough to make crevices between them. They looked like what I imagined a gully to be. But sort of bouncy and shy.

I traced a really long ruffle that wound almost the entire way round Mum's cave. It was massive. And thin. And squiggly. And so, so beautiful. I wanted to touch it, so I wiggled myself into the cave a bit more. This made me bigger. Rounder. I felt good cause I was most probably growing up. Getting fat. The way a baby should.

Soon, coldness crept into me.

I turned to see where it was coming from. Right at the edge of my growing blob was a splotch. It was smallish and uneven. The splodge's centre was a mix of white and a sicky grey. And its surface was scratchy. Nothing like the flowing softness of everywhere else in Mum's cave.

The splat dissolved into weakish twists, its outskirts kind of like a useless limb or something. These bits didn't hold or grab or push away. They seemed too hopeless for that. They just sort of hung there. Looking at the whole scuffed-up, weak-limbed blotch, I decided it was probably a sigh.

I brushed against its dead little toes and it sent icy bolts into me. Each jolt of cold made me jump. It was yuck cause everything else around me was warm and soft. I tried to edge away but new sparks kept reaching and entering me. The more I wobbled away from it, the more desperate the cold bolts became. They flew at me non-stop.

I tried to dodge them. I wobbled a lot. And squirmed away as best I could. But that really only made me bigger and the space between us smaller.

The longer I spread over the splat, the less hurty and cutting the cold blasts became. I got used to it, I guess. Soon I globuled over its centre. Feeling its grossish face made me feel even sorrier for it. It was nothing more than a sorrow splat. Then I felt really bad for trying to escape it. I also felt bad I was squashing it.

'Hello,' I said. 'I hope I'm not hurting you.'

There was no reply.

'And sorry for being a bit jumpy,' I said, a bit louder. 'I'm only new. I'm still trying to get the hang of things.' I thought that was pretty funny. Nothing else seemed to though.

'If you're still cold, I can squish over you a bit more. If you think that will help?' I expanded. Then collapsed even further, covering all the cold splodge's fibrous face. I wiggled around on it, thinking maybe the rubbing might wake it. Or warm it up. Or something like that. But all I could hear was the swishing of Mum cave water. And the occasional belly gargle. I worked out it most probably couldn't talk. So, I spoke to myself after that.

'I'll just hang out here, if that's alright. The rest of me will have to come though at some stage.' I hoped I was right. I couldn't be sure.

I decided to hug the cold splat while I waited. I figured it was probably a nice thing to do. I imagined cupping hands to my mouth and blowing warm air onto them. Then I imagined placing my palms and spread-out fingers across the icy splat. Moments after, the pore I was seeping through let go of my ankle bits. At least that's what I supposed they were. I guess I was right, cause I felt feet spaces start to grow. They tingled as I floated around Mum's cave. It felt sad and weird and exciting, tumbling away from the cold graze and further into Mum's thick goo.

A pulse rang though the cave. It was a regular double pump. Short, full. Da, dum. Ba, boom. Its rhythm filled me. The sound was around me as well as inside me at the same time. I guess I became it. Or it became me. I got used to it being an always thing. A warm happiness spread through me as I pulsed and drifted inside a squishy, warm mum. Becoming a baby seemed like a sweet, floaty deal just then. I hoped this was all there was to growing into a baby and getting born.

20.

Everything went meltish and turned me cosy-drowsy. This triggered a series of zooming people faces that folded into my eye bits. It must have been my first ever dream. Old people, children, what were probably aunties and grandfathers and cousins and things. I only think that because somehow the idea they were my family came with them. It stuck to them. Or flew with them as they rushed me. The faces were non-stop. One after the other. Not panicky or worryish. Or wanting to speak even. They were just steady. Looking at me. Wanting to be seen. They all stared straight into my centre as they paraded into me. I didn't introduce myself or offer them a word. I had no time to say anything. All I had was space to look back at them as they passed by.

After the longest time, the parade started to make me tired. I felt heavy cause I was putting in a lot of effort making sure the faces saw me watching. But getting tired just made them come even faster.

Then I went wobbly and everything went black.

'Sprite?'

The voice was strong and clear. Also kind sounding.

I tried meeting it. When I searched for a face in the dark of Mum's cave, I straight away saw an outline of the cold splat. Her voice was a girl's. I imagined her long and skinny. Nothing like the cold splatter I nudged against when I'd started growing just before.

'Me?' I asked the darkness.

'You're Sprite, aren't you?' she said, questioning.

'I'm ...' I didn't know what word to say next.

She laughed. I knew she was peering at my egg.

'Go on,' she prompted, a little tease dancing inside her words.

'I'm ... I've ... I'm here.' It was the best I could do. I deflated a bit. Mum's beeps pounded in my closed hearing parts.

'I can see,' the voice said. 'I've been waiting for you for a long time, Sprite.'

'You have?' My insides bounced their own pattern of beeps when I heard that. The thudding made me a bit dizzy. I thought I would pass out. Again. She laughed at me. Probably cause I was turning green.

'Don't fight it, Sprite. It's a good thing.'

I was trying hard not to panic. It mustn't have been working.

She added, 'Let Mum help. She's good at that.'

So, I sucked in a big gulp of mum water. The girl was right. My rushings calmed down.

'Thank you. What do I call you?'

'I'm a dream. You can call me that or make up a new name! I don't mind. Up to you, Sprite!' she said lightly.

She made me feel good. Words rushed out. I didn't even know I was going to make them. 'You're that Cold Scar, aren't you?' I knew I was right cause, as soon as I said it, her face graze came into my inside thought place.

'I'm that scar's memory.'

I didn't know anything about how scars worked or what a memory even was, so I got a bit confused then. She could probably tell.

'It's an echo,' she added. 'I'm an echo.'

I scrunched up my face parts trying to sort through all the new bits.

'That's okay. You don't have to get it. There's plenty of time for that.'

Even though she appeared as a darkness, I knew colours were flying around her as she spoke-thought. 'You concentrate on being yourself, Sprite. Whatever that is. It'll be more than enough for us.' Her words were paintings. I loved every one of them.

I asked her why she was a wound. She smiled, then said scars are special because they're the way a woman's body talked. She told me for men it's a bit different. They mostly marked themselves on purpose to show how courageous they were. When I asked her what courageous meant she said brave. She told me that my mum carried babies and that's where the scars came from. When I asked if I'd make a scar on Mum, she said yes. I felt bad then. But she said scars are a mum's way of never forgetting her children. She said now I was here, Mum would get happier cause she wouldn't spend as much time thinking about and missing her babies that had gone.

Cold Scar took up a part of my shell that might one day become a hand. I felt melty because, all of a sudden, the dream that was a memory and an echo at the same time became an actual thing I could feel. When I looked at where we connected, I noticed half her pointy finger was missing. I wanted to ask her about it, but I was worried it was a sad thing. So I didn't. I kept quiet and tried to let her know I was squeezing her. Not in an angry way but with a soft kindness.

'There are also scars you can't see, Sprite. Try and remember that,' Cold Scar told me. 'They're invisible. Never on the outside,' she said, turning me around nodding deeper into Mum's cave.

'They make things rude, and nasty sometimes,' she said. 'Be patient, Sprite. And loving.'

I told her I didn't know what loving was yet. She said it was just being kind, even when it was hard. I thought that sounded tough to do, but I promised I'd try. For her.

She told me how happy she was that I'd come, that she had the chance to talk to me by herself for a little while. And she was pleased that I was to spend time with Mum and whoever else came along.

'It will be good for everyone,' she said.

When I asked her if she had felt me trying to keep her warm inside Mum's cave, she said that she had. She thanked me. But even though she was a scar in Mum's belly, and talking to me now, she was somewhere else as well. In a few different places at once, most times.

'Like this dream, little Sprite,' she said to me. 'Here and nowhere all at once.'

Before she left, I asked her if I'd ever see her or hold her hand again. She didn't answer exactly. She just said I had lots of life to live, and I should try to do it the best way I could. She made her darkness smile at me then. I felt it push waves of purple and pink and a bit of bright orange inside me. And then she faded. Or I fell asleep for the first time ever. I can't say which.

21.

What happened next was a lot of churning. And being chucked about. I cannoned over every place of Mum's entire cave. The bounces were hard and sharp, and I was slapped into her lining. I must have slammed into every part of her. And because I was in one and having a hard time of it, I think I got my own tummy then.

I started to feel sick. A lot. Spasms and heaves whacked me all over the place and I couldn't tell if it was my guts or Mum's cramping that was the problem. And all the flinging made me worry that she might hate me before she met me cause I was making her sick too. So, I tried to soften myself. Flatten my roundness to cushion some of the blows.

Eventually the whacks became slower, because I was getting heavier. My splodge site spread until I basically began bobbing. I glooped around her in a tired side-to-side.

Getting big pushed me deeper into the curtains and ruffles of Mum's cave lining.

Soon my weight brought me to a stop and plonked me firmly in her side. It felt nice to be cuddled by her belly folds, so I tried to cuddle back. I felt a sort of buzzing where arms might grow, so I pressed it against her hoping she could feel my embrace. As I did, I lolloped into a ditch bit. One side was all folds and softness, but the other part was harsh. The scuff was wide and uneven. But warm.

This was a different scar. It had an elevated centre crater. I guess it was a face. Its middle was crisscrossy. Tough and tight. Sort of angry. Or hurt. I couldn't tell which. And this one was a weird colour. It was pale. If I had eyes, they might have told me this splat was a stainy sick yellow. With fine red veins. But my eyes weren't there yet, so it was just my thoughts or inside knowing that told me.

The scar had freaky little finger claws that gripped but also pushed at Mum's regular insides, mucking up the cuddly ruffles of Mum's belly. But its yucko claws and scratched-up, weird colour face told me for sure it was a scar. Just like Cold Scar. A wound. Then I got a bit sad that there were two scars. And that they were so far apart. One was way up high in Mum's belly and the other one was all the way down here and they couldn't hold each other. Scars needed friends too.

I breathed out and spilled onto its edges a bit, mainly to see if it would talk. I wriggled on it. Its beat matched Mum's. But softer. Like a buried breath or something.

'Hello,' I said, waiting.

There was no reply.

Cause I was starting to get tired, I thought about giving up just then. But I didn't want to seem rude.

'I really like your … claws.' I said, trying to smile.

Mum's belly gurgled.

'I'm not really sure what I'm sposed to do now,' I continued. 'I don't even know how to sleep. Or if I should rest or explore a bit. I don't know anything about how bodies work,' I said, wincing. 'Which is not good since I'm in one and growing one at the same time.'

I waited. Still nothing.

'Hopefully, someone will give me instructions.'

It was completely quiet. Apart from mum gurgles.

I realised then that talking to myself hoping a scar might speak back was silly. And that now I was in a mum cave and trying to work out how to become a baby, I was probably going to be useless at it.

I kept talking though, more for myself than anyone else. 'You probably didn't see but just to get here I was swished around a bit then squeezed through a tiny roof hole, then shot with ice zaps. I've only just stopped zinging off the walls.' I wiggled again. 'But you're here, so you would have done it all already,' I said. 'I guess.'

Just then a burning flash of heat ignited beneath me, right where I touched the scar. It made me jump.

'Aww,' I screamed. 'What the heck?'

Still nothing.

I gathered myself as much as I could away from the scar's outer patches. It took a lot of effort to be tensed up and away from it, cause it was so everywhere. But I didn't want any more surprises. I kept tight and still. It wasn't relaxing at all.

I gave up talking too. I concentrated on taking gulps of mum water and letting it swirl inside me. I listened to the swooshing of Mum's beat and the creaks and gargles of her cave. They were a little bit gross to begin with. Mainly cause of how wet and icky warm they sounded. But after a while the rumblings and churnings of my mum turned into music. Keeping myself bundled away from the burning scar, I folded into the stillness and let that belly song grow me up a bit.

22.

No Man's Corner

Ginny scanned her kitchen's bashed-up metal sink. From her seat at the table, she counted five used, unwashed mugs. Toast-crumbed dishes multiplied and overflowed onto the bench top. She didn't bother counting them, there were too many. Even so, she knew there were probably a couple more under her bed. Alongside an array of metal spoons and plastic forks and takeaway containers. *I'll have to do a big clean up*, she thought, looking out her open front door. 'But not today,' she said, jumping up and flinging her jacket on, then flying down her stairs.

She walked towards a dilapidated, abandoned house she called 'no man's corner'. It was uneasily nestled into a corner block just off the end of her street. Ginny often went there whenever she needed space. Or inspiration. Or distraction. For her, the collapsing sandstone brickwork and boarded-up windows of the once grand property were magnetic. A porthole-esque window near the front entrance sported luscious, red stained-glass flowers spilling from an elegant green vase. The door's paint was grey and blistered. Three windows atop the cracked stone steps suggested a front drawing room oriented directly towards the centre of the intersecting roads outside. The overgrown lawn was dominated by a scraggle of Birds of Paradise thicket and lantana. Graffiti was sprayed across the two modern brick fences. The house proper concluded in a succession of plyboard and cracked glass, its fibro extension of corrugated iron and plastic sheeting a direct contrast to its federation frontage. A scraggle of forgotten greenery separated the house from its detached garage, Boston Fern sprouting through the cracked concrete. The house's exterior confirmed Ginny's suspicion that it was totally abandoned. Unclaimed. Unloved. Yet one dusk evening, coming back from yoga, she had noticed a light inside. A light meant eyes. Eyes meant squatters. This made the overflowing letterbox, the continuing brokenness, the ignored cracks and foundation shifts all the more intriguing. Ginny reasoned it had to be electricity, not a caved-in section of ceiling, that provided the light. It glowed from deep within the bowels of the house.

All the inconsistences, all the bits that had fallen away or out or didn't fit, for Ginny, made the place irresistible.

Scanning its falling-down story was way better than doing her dishes. And a middle of the day visit was as good a moment as any.

She made quick time to the park that marked the halfway point between her flat and deserted house. A middle-aged couple sat on one of the benches sipping their coffee in the sun. Ginny nodded then kept on, past the sprawling banksia and over a run of fresh, white concrete, then turned into the stunted street towards the house. The block, at the junction of a train line and two sleepy, suburban streets, had no dwellings on its opposite side. Its neighbouring properties were a mixture of freshly renovated terraces – more designer ship container than home. The types that lived in these were workaholics – had to be, considering the market – and were beavering away till all hours. They had no kids with nosy grandparents or dogs to set off an intruder alert. Ginny fancied she'd try to find a way in. At the very least, one glance of its kitchen would put her own domestic disorganisation into some perspective. A smug looking cat stretched against the warm concrete a few doors away from the house. It didn't flinch as she approached. She stomped hard, hoping to shoo it away and clear her path, but the tabby only raised its head and curled the tip of its extended tail as she tiptoed around it. She didn't like cats so she chucked a sharp hiss at it as she passed. It was an easy approach to the building from the backyard but she decided to walk its perimeter first to check for any signs of life inside. That would be another thing, she thought, as she skirted the fence. Something she hadn't considered. What if there was a shrivelled-up, mummified body in there, or a half-buried someone in the falling-down fireplace or something? Or worse, a wired-up druggo. If there was, she reasoned, she'd have a quick stickybeak from a safe distance then, depending on the state of the inhabitant, either anonymously call it in at the phone booth near the fish and chip shop or go get a coffee and chocolate croissant round the corner. 'Easy,' she told herself, leering past the front door towards the place she had spotted the indoor light. Inside seemed dark. And lifeless. 'Just act like you own it,' she said, approaching the hollow gate and unlatching it. 'Seems to be the go round here.'

Ginny swung open the gate, surprised by its fluidity. She noticed rust infestations all throughout the fence joins. After ascending the handful of marble stairs of the front entrance, Ginny strode along the veranda to the front door. She thought she could just make out a geometric pattern in the tiles beneath her feet, but dirt and moss had overridden its vibrance. Approaching the front door, she felt unusually calm. Confident almost. 'Like a cat,' she laughed to herself. Ginny looked hard at the entrance. The white door was panelled but plain. The doorbell had been painted over long ago. As had an undersized doorknob. She grasped it, then looked above her. The roof of the veranda directly above it was caving in and peeling away, its painted green wood buckling and splitting while managing, miraculously, to remain aloft. Quickly, Ginny turned the door handle. Expecting it to be jammed, or immovably caked shut. She gasped as it clicked and glided open. Pushing the door, Ginny stepped inside.

The dark interior smelled of dirt. And mould. Dust and unkempt habitation had given way to substantial holding, growing deposits of earth. It was musty and organic and alive. She closed the door behind her. It clicked shut. Carefully, Ginny inched along the wooden floorboards. They creaked under her as she crept along the hallway in the dim light. She peered around the first doorway to her right. Sun angled in through the three windows, illuminating a tilted square of floor at the feet of their frame. Not far away, towards the corner of the oddly oriented room, was the only piece of furniture. It was an armchair, its once lime green velvet covering now patchy and threadbare. Ginny walked towards it. At its base, candle stubs, like melted tree trunks, were stuck to the floor. A handful of books – old volumes with thick, dark leather spines – lay open around the candles. Ginny knelt next to them to read their titles.

Crouching close, she noticed the stuffing of the armchair had collapsed, its wiry filling and internal springs spillling onto the floor. A squeak came from the tangle. Ginny jumped up and bolted out of the room and into the hall.

The next room held a heavy wooden wardrobe. An elongated mirror that had occupied the facade of one of its doors had disappeared and its top edge was skewed and collapsing. Moving towards it, Ginny spotted an empty bed frame. Its wood was light and still sturdy. Its bare base was a concentrated mesh of close wire coils, almost like chain. Walking towards it, Ginny noticed a single mattress on the floor beneath the window. Sheets of old newspaper had been laid between mattress and floorboards, and a mangled doona was heaped beside it on the floor. She leaned down, inspecting the slight depression in the bed. She hovered an outstretched palm over it, then laughed at herself. 'I'm a tracker all of a sudden.' She stood, looking from the window into the backyard. 'Trespasser, more like. How ironic.'

She continued past what she supposed were more bedrooms and towards the brightest part of the house. It was near the back entrance and looked out onto the wild garden she had so many times traced on her way past. The long bricked kitchen was an appendage to the rest of the house. A cement trough with two taps protruded from the wall. A makeshift bench had been shoved in beside. A greying wood table rested against the opposing wall. Two chairs, their backs flush with the wall, were at either end. Plyboard acted as insulator against the outdoors, three grey lace curtains draping over the weathered boards. A mismatched, ill-fitting door blocked off an enclosed atrium at the far end of the room. Ginny looked on the table. A mug was plonked in front of the furthest chair. She shuffled beside the kitchen bench. An open packet of Scotch Finger biscuits rested on the bench. Ginny scanned the surrounds. A rounded fridge, impossibly old fashioned, was plonked near the back exit. She strained, listening for a whirring compressor. The annex remained silent. A train rumbled along the not-too-distant track. Ginny made her way to the nearest chair and sat down. There were clear signs of life yet no body nor breath. The house was both occupied and empty, loud with living yet silent. She closed her eyes and rest her head against the brick wall.

'You the owner?' said a gravelly, dry voice.

Ginny opened her eyes. A man shuffled towards her from the vestibule. She sat bolt upright. His thin hair and thick whiskers beamed white. The man sat then smiled at her. Immediately Ginny noticed his front tooth was missing. She stared at the gap. Smiling, his tongue traced the gum of the missing space.

'Well, are ya?'

'Am I what?' she replied, still unable to take her eyes off his teeth. Or lack thereof.

'The owner? Of this?' The man flung his arm into the room. 'Look like you might be.'

Ginny shrugged. Tension released from her shoulders, making the rest of her body relax. She shifted in the chair.

'Well, owner, I've had a good run.' The man winked. 'So good in fact, I can claim squatter's rights.'

Ginny watched as Squatter Man extended his legs, crossed them at the ankles and rested his head on his hands.

'*Terra nullius*, I believe, is the correct term.'

'Yeah,' scoffed Ginny, 'replaced by its current name, *a legal fiction*, by Eddie Mabo. Nineteen ninety-two, I believe.'

'You're a quick one. Saw you come in by the way. Bold.'

Ginny nodded and grinned.

'So, your lot gunna let me stay? Wouldn't want to have to take you to court. Squatter's rights and all that.'

'Why should we?' Ginny rallied.

'What choice do you have?' The man replied, straightening. 'You can't take care of it like you used to, not like I can in any case.'

'Yeah,' Ginny laughed back, 'Obviously.'

'Look,' he said, flicking an imaginary speck of dust from his jumper sleeve, dandruff and dead skin cascading from his head and face. 'I'll do my best to look after things. Keep it the way you like. I'm doing you a favour, really. Upkeep on a place like this is way beyond your capabilities.'

Ginny looked at the peeling paint, curling in sad arches away from the ceiling. A line of ants crawled from the fault in the wall towards the Scotch Fingers.

'Let's ... just ... park it for now,' said Squatter Man, rising. 'I need to show you something, come with me.' He shuffled past Ginny and down the hallway. Squatter Man went into a room and towards some loose bricks in its wall. He waved Ginny closer. 'Don't worry,' he said, running his hands over the wall. 'I'm not going to pull out a body.'

He removed two bricks and reached into the crevice. 'What do you know about love?' Squatter Man asked, as he extracted a cupped hand.

'What can you ever know about it?' Ginny replied, leaning towards the small item he cradled in his palm.

'Not much, you're right. One of life's true mysteries.' He went on. 'But when we pull back from its object, the absence of love reveals parts of ourselves we never knew existed. If we are repairing and ready to see.' The man smiled, his gummy gap glistening. Tenderly, he opened his hand and held it out to Ginny. An oval frame encircled a sepia photograph. The portrait was of a woman holding a gentle smile. Her dark, shoulder-length curls fell onto a delicate, collared blouse. 'I held on too long. I lost myself inside stories of hope. And fancy. And what should have been. When it started to crumble, I propped up the beams. Yearning more than anything to be the lover I was when with her. To become the person she drew out of me. But it ended. We ended. And I was lost. I tried everything to patch the holes. But I became consumed by my brokenness.' The man nudged Ginny. She nodded then winced. He continued. 'Only when I allowed love to be over could I disintegrate. I didn't expect my foundations to survive. But they did. And that meant I could renovate,' he said cheekily, nudging her a little harder this time. Ginny smiled. 'Improvements, extensions built me back to love again. Or a version at least. Grateful. For all I had received, as short and as precious as it was. Thankful, in my heartbreak, for its gift rather than grief-stricken at its premature loss.' Squatter Man looked at the picture then fingered the outline of the softly grinning woman. 'All the tendernesses and kindnesses and attention you gave were beautiful gifts that enriched my life. Thank you.' Squatter Man kissed the photo, then returned it to its place within the crumbling wall. He turned to Ginny. 'Don't let your estate get beyond repair. That doesn't honour any inheritance.'

The man walked towards the front door. Ginny followed.

'So, what do ya say? Extend the lease?'

'Spose so,' she said.

'Won't increase the rent?' he asked her.

'Not today,' Ginny said. 'But I do want this,' she added, spotting a fallen fly screen from a second set of drawing room windows. 'As bond.'

'Take it,' said Squatter Man. 'What do you want it for?'

Ginny pulled the mesh off the frame, then rolled the netting against her thigh. 'For … repossession purposes. Landowner stuff.' Ginny opened the door and stepped onto the veranda.

'Smooth sailing,' Squatter Man called to her as she bounded down the stairs.

Ginny turned and saluted. With her scroll tucked safely under her arm, she made her way home.

23.

Something heated whacked my side.
I wobbled awake.

'Knock it off, will ya!' the voice said.

'Huh?' I couldn't see what was going on, so I moved to the side, away from the hurt. My under-butt bit stung. I could feel warmth pulsate thorough the ruffles of Mum's cave wall. I tried to get comfy, but it was a rough, scratchy heat, not a cosy, hugging one.

'Great! So not only do you snore, you also wiggle. Non-stop.'

'Who's there?' I said, trying to search Mum's tummy curtains for some clue about what was going on.

'Are you going to be like this the entire time?' a voice squealed.

I knew then who it was. I matched the sound to the face.

Or in this case, the scar. The warm second scar on Mum's belly sounded exactly the way he looked.

'I definitely wasn't snoring, cause I don't know how to sleep ye—'

'Here's the deal,' he squeaked. 'Stay still. And quiet. If you can't …' He bristled. 'Push off somewhere else.' He tried to force me off him. I jiggled a bit but returned to the exact same place.

'That's a bit rude,' I told him.

'My cave, my rules.'

'How is it your—'

'Quiet!'

'But—'

'Shh,' he hissed. It was harsh and I knew it was spitty even though we already floated in Mum juice.

I collected myself into a tighter ball. 'You're not that welcoming,' I said.

He laughed. It was uneven and jutty and all over the place. I realised then he was still part boy. Nowhere near a full man scar yet.

'What's so funny?' I asked, angrily. Then I wondered if a bit of him had rubbed off on me when I'd been asleep.

'You are,' he squawked. I could tell he was shaking his head part, even though his face was only a pile of scratches.

'You didn't tell me he was this nasty,' I yelled up to Cold Scar.

'She's not even there,' he went on. 'You're talking to yourself.' He chucked a cackle into the centre of Mum's cave. 'And waiting for an answer. How stupid!'

'That's how little you know,' I snapped back.

'Oh,' he teased. 'Who's being rude now, little Miss Waiting-to-be-born?'

He was right. So, I tried at being a bit softer. Even though I didn't really want to.

'I had a lovely talk to …' I searched for the right order of words. It was important I got it right in front of this Boy Scar. 'Sister. Cold Scar,' I added, firmly.

Just then I remembered my promise to her. I told her I'd try to be patient. And kind. So tried making myself sound little. Light. 'She says she loves you,' I said, even though she didn't. I thought it might help me, so I went with it. 'She also wanted me to ask for your help to figure out how to be in a mum,' I said. I looked at him but knew his back was turned. 'I'd really love some—'

'Quiet!' he shrieked. The end of his word grew a tail and shook itself into a weird squeal. It sounded funny, floating around and echoing in all the mum water. It was also very rude. I was trying to be nice to this nasty Boy Scar.

So, I laughed. I made sure to make my imaginary shoulder bones bounce with the effort as I did. Then a sharp sting whacked into my side behind bit. Halfway down. Until then I hadn't known that part of me. Now I knew it was meaty and tender. The stab ached then began heat-pulsing. I thought I might spew up.

'Don't even,' Boy Scar warned. Then he mind-kicked me in another tender bit on the opposite side. I didn't have fingers but I managed to grab him then twist. I held as tight as I could, then squeezed harder. The scar began to screech.

'Who's wriggling now?' I said. 'What are you squeaking about?' I yelled then, cause a boy who was a scar who hurt little beginning babies was nothing to be scared of.

I felt him wangle free. Somehow. My new finger places buzzed, like they knew what they were going to be and were ready for some serious growing.

'Listen you … what are you?' he baulked. 'A boil? A zit? Or are you a silly little spit ball that's probably not even wanted?' He made himself wider. His scar tensed and he rose from Mum's lining. 'She'll be so disappointed you're a dumb-dumb.' He scoff-snorted. That made my skin slither. Or what I imagined was skin, anyway. I must have made a face. Don't know how. Cause he got angrier.

'We will get on fine,' he said meanishly. 'If you do like I say and sit still and shut up!'

160

'You can't talk—'

'Just so happens I'm doing you a favour,' he jutted back. 'If you can't do as you're told here, Mum won't be too pleased.'

'Thought you said she wasn't even here.' I looked to Cold Scar, still grey and lifeless. I liked her so much more.

'Not her, you dumb little speck.'

'Who then, Scratch Face?' This scar was the pits. He was making me hate him.

'Who do you think?' I could hear in his ugly singing talk that he was enjoying making me annoyed. 'Your mum, of course.'

I felt my inside water fizz. 'What would you know about my mum?' I blurted back.

'I'm here, aren't I?' he spat. 'And well before you too! You work it out.'

My insides heated up. When it mixed with all the fizzing I was already doing, I thought for sure I would spew up. That's probably when my belly juices must have come in.

Boy Scar was tense and still sitting high, but I guess he didn't want me to chuck all over him. 'Look,' he said a bit softer. 'You need to get used to how things are in here,' he said. 'Looks like we're stuck with each other.'

His rim fluttered down a bit. It softened into Mum's pink belly folds.

'Just be patient. And quiet if you can. Please,' he added. 'Something is bound to happen to get you out of here. In time.' He did a long sigh after that. I thought about feeling sad for him. But I decided not to. Cold Scar was so much nicer to me when we first met.

'What am I waiting for?' I asked.

He didn't answer. But his ignoring wasn't cold or nasty rude anymore.

I relaxed a bit and let my outside rest lightly on the lip of Boy Scar. I imagined my hand on top of his. Even though he was right next to me, and I was snuggled a bit into his warmness, I could tell he had somehow gone. Drifted away.

Mum's belly got echoey again. Muffled, garglish gut noises sounded throughout her cave. I tried to snuggle into Boy Scar. He didn't shove me off this time. But he was tight. And hard. We felt so different from each other.

'How will I ever get the hang of this?' I said to myself. 'I'm not even a baby. I'm just a blob.'

'Spit, actually,' came the reply, a thought from Boy Scar sent a really, really long time later. 'You're Spit. For now.'

24.

'C'mon. Up you get.'

I was being shaken and Mum's belly ruffles were making rolly waves inside her gut. I tried to squish myself into one of her pillowy crevices. Most of me was wobbling.

'Little Spitty Splat,' Boy Scar sang, rattling me around.

'Will you stop? My name is Sprite,' I whinged. He was really jolting me around now and I was still only small. It took all the strength I had to keep pushed into one spot.

'You have to wake up.'

'I'm always awake,' I told him.

'You don't look it,' he said back. 'All droopy and floppish.' He sounded light. 'I've decided to take you on.'

'I don't know how to sleep yet,' I replied. 'And take me on what?'

He thrust himself upwards, rising from Mum's folds. It stopped all the jerking. 'Only the most important part of your splatty life so far.'

I liked him this way. He was different. Playful. Not so sorrowish and annoying. I figured if I kept asking questions, he might stay that way. 'Huh?' I said.

'Spit,' he announced, smiling, 'I am going to teach you everything you need to know before you are a born baby.'

My insides cartwheeled. 'Everything?' I asked, trying to urge my eye sockets to bloom. 'Really?'

'Well, mostly everything,' he added. 'There'll be things I can't be bothered with of course. Mostly girlish stuff like lady ways and feelings. And anything that takes too much talking. We won't be wasting time with that.'

'Okay.' It was all I could think to say then.

'I have worked out,' he continued, beginning to strut, invisible hands held behind his imaginary back, 'it's in your best interests, Spit, to know things when you are born and not just come out a dumb girl baby.' He made himself bigger, how I don't know. 'I can help you with that. I *will* help you,' he corrected. 'And you're very lucky,' he said bouncily, 'cause I will be a very, very good teacher.' He paused. 'The best in fact!'

'So, you've done this before?'

He stopped moving and shot me a side look but didn't answer.

'Let's begin,' he squeaked, then cleared the boyishness from his throat. 'Mum will expect a lot from you. Because of her, we have a special—'

'We're special?' I sprang in, excited we were starting straight away.

'Hey,' he warned, holding a finger to his lips. He walked a few steps, then waved the same finger before him as he continued. 'She'll want you to come out knowing a lot of stuff. So you're clever. Like us. So, I want your full attention.' He stared at me. 'First, she'll never want you to ask a question you don't know the answer to. That's what she'll say. Sometime after you get born.'

'But if she's going to tell me that anyway, why do I need to know that now?'

'Shh,' he hissed. 'And only speak when you're spoken to.'

I stayed quiet to prove how good a student I was going to be.

'Well, Spit, do you understand? Or are you going to be a bit slow?'

'You just tol—'

'Oh, and it's rude to keep people waiting. That's another thing she'll want you to know. And you've already mucked that one up, haven't you?' He continued to pace, thinking hard into the ruffles before him.

'How?' I said.

He pointed to the roof of Mum's cave. Right near where Cold Scar was. When I looked up there, I gave her a little wave.

'Oi,' he said, bringing my attention back to him. 'You dangled there for ages before you fell. Then you banged all over Mum's cave without caring what you whacked. Also girls should never talk back,' he added. 'That's another thing you will definitely need to know.'

'You made that one up.' I said. 'And it wasn't my choice to—'

Boy Scar stopped. He towered over me. His eyes went right into my chest. I could feel it starting to get hot.

'Bang around,' I finished, unable to help it.

'That's it!' he boomed. 'Knew it was a bad idea,' he said, shaking his head. 'You don't want to learn anything. And guess what?' He heaved as he shuddered, 'Mum's not gunna like you sliding out like a jellyfish. She hates em cause they're all wobbles and no spine.'

I thought about telling him to shut up. Then lying and saying it was only a joke. Then I thought I might tell him off for being mean and bossy, and for not teaching me in the right way. I could also say no way was I a jellyfish, even though I didn't know what a jellyfish was. I tried to make the picture of one in my mind. What came was a fluffy, blobbish glob that smiled and showed three sharp teeth.

I gazed into the centre of Mum's cave. I figured it made me sad looking. 'I'm sorry,' I said, making my voice soft. Just then I thought maybe a jellyfish was just words with floppy sounding edges.

'I don't have ears yet so—' I stopped. Then tried again. 'I promise from now on I'll listen. I'll gulp in everything you say and swish it down with mum water,' I added. 'So you can both swirl around inside of me. Showing me how to grow. Would that be alright with you?'

Mum's beat made a really strong banging sound just then. Boy Scar looked around Mum's cave and put his head down a bit. I think a tear came out of his graze. Maybe a jellyfish was not a creature or word at all.

'If you keep going, I'll get better at listening. And when I'm born and breathing air and starting to become an outside, grown-up baby, you will be outside with me. I won't be alone or frightened then. Can you keep teaching and growing me up, please?'

I could feel his beats push harder. It copied Mum's strong taps and was warm and full. It felt nice. Close.

He sort of melted back into what he always was.

'We might have more luck if we try again tomorrow, little Spit.'

'What's tomorrow?' I asked.

'The time after Mum rests. Tomorrow is when she will wake up.'

I could feel him shutting down, disappearing from me.

'Thank you,' I called to him. 'And sorry,' I said. 'I'll be better. And ready! For tomorrow.'

As he dissolved into the ruffles of Mum's lining, I heard him squeak a handful of sad little cries. He sucked up some snot then went quiet again. When I peered over his turned shoulder, Boy Scar had become invisible amongst Mum's folds.

I wanted to copy him, so I let my blob spread, seeing if I could melt myself into her. Nothing happened. So I waited, maybe the way a jellyfish would.

25.

Dreaming-continuous

Ginny leaned into her heels. It had been an age since she had felt the road's sheerness push into her. Over time she had tentatively begun to revisit some of her and Nathan's old routes, but until now she had avoided the Unwin Street hill. Knowing the twin homes perched on its corner were finished made Ginny eager to see them. And by now, surely, she'd be strong enough to leave and ascend Unwin's slope safely.

As she followed the road's curve, the tension in her kneecaps built. Ginny's steps shortened, transforming into shuffle. She clenched her abs. It assisted in the slow decline. Her unsteady steps allowed a reacquaintance with details she knew well but had forgotten. The vacant lot hadn't changed. It was still encaged by its rickety fence, the accompanying chain still thick and gleaming. The fading, plastic, red and white tape that cordoned off the lot still twirled in the breezes that lifted from the creek. And the signage for the community garden and asbestos detection agency both clung lopsided from the chain wire fence. The grime-splattered fishing boat remained on the slope outside number sixty-two, thanks to a pile of mould-caked bricks and stodgy wooden wedges. Ginny's skin tingled and cheeks flushed as she remembered Nathan leaping into the cabin then jumping on its bow.

The hill's rise gave a perfect platform from which to witness the meeting of creek and river. Water wound around the flatness – sporting fields and parks now pressed into old floodplains – and forced slowness into the heaving city surrounds. The reconstructed bushland of the foreshore swallowed the concrete. Train lines and revving cars were forced to navigate around the water, shaping curls and bends into the cement and steel. From halfway up the steep street, the city's modern-day music channelled into her. Sustained and constant, the urban drone entered through her soles and stopped at her gut to resonate. Crescendo-ing to fullness, it escaped through her hair. She inhaled. The breath's salty tail hit the back of her tongue and she swallowed. Sprawling chaotic stillness grasped at her throat, the energy and tranquillity of the hill making her neck muscles seize. All around was glorious. And menacing. Ancient and unborn. From that point on the hill, braced against the weight of the slope, Ginny felt all the world's new foreignness, and every part of her belonging. It was beautiful.

Continuing, Ginny looked to the sprawling white tower with green cross beams that dominated the opposing shore. A corner unit had been her dream. A distant, secret one. She had spent hours imagining how life high above the freeway, nuzzled into the forking of creek and river, might be for her. Sunrise could kiss the keyboard of her laptop good morning and midday may perhaps unlock a sentence amongst the flow. She was certain the doubtless white shelving would enhance the colour of her expanding collection of notebooks. She dared to hope that, with each extraction and insertion, her stories and language and craft would grow. She would never let the sunroom become clogged with fit balls and pushbikes and other ill-thought-out, well-intentioned clutter of city life. Not like everyone else. That would be her writing room. Where the thin shyness of the boulder-hemmed creek would dip her words in wisdom. And the bold river would push movement and vigour onto her page. The sun-come-writing room would be where Nathan would place mugs of freshly made coffee next to plates of toast and apricot jam. It would also be the room where, at the end of full days, they might sit on the floor and eat green curry with boiled rice and watch the reflection of lights from the airport flicker and sway.

As Ginny further descended, the heft of the apartment block disappeared into the mangroves. She never did tell Nathan about his role in her dream, even in their most love-soaked walks past the units where, for hours, they ferreted amongst the mudflats along the creek's eroded banks. It was too intimate. It hurt just to hold.

Her steps lengthened with the softening angle of the street. Ginny's hand went to the side of her gym pants. The poem was still wedged, folded tight in the pocket of her tights. She curled away from the bitumen and crunched along the gravel of the waterside path. After hurdling a clump of Lomandra, she came to the small landslide that had cleared a path to the water. Her intention was to scramble to the waterline and jam the poem amongst the palm-sized oyster shells imbedded in the mud. All this she would expertly do without dirtying her favourite pair of runners. Then she would take a look at the new houses on the corner. They would tell her how long it had been. How far she had come. They would show her the process of rebuilding was worth it in the end. Then Ginny planned to attack the hill, sprint up it, and make her way home. But she was taken aback by the steady trickle of people along the walkway. It was unusual for it to be so busy there.

She poked her head up the bank a bit. An A frame sign was propped out the front of the corner house. Couples, mostly, approached and walked inside. Ginny looked at the muck of the waterline. Then to her shoes. In three big strides, she was back on the path and following the steady, human stream into the house.

Its facade was grey. And blockish. Dusted white concrete set off the deep slate of the entrance steps. She walked through the doorway and along a white corridor. Its tan floorboards opened out into a wide living room. Black French windows framed the trumpeting green of the sporting fields on the other side of the road.

A woman with a short, blonde bob sprung seemingly from nowhere. 'Welcome.'

Ginny jumped. 'Oh, hi.'

'Here for the inspection?' she said, her sentence slowing as she spoke.

'Sure,' Ginny replied. 'Why not?'

The woman pushed out a tight, synthetic smile. 'Feel free to have a look around.' She took her in. 'And let me know if you have any questions.' Her gaze dropped and lingered on Ginny's upper belly flab.

'When was it finished?' Ginny asked.

'I beg your pardon,' the woman replied, now staring at Ginny's cleavage, which was bursting out and over her cheap and most comfortable sports bra.

'When was the building completed?'

'Only last week. And it won't stay on the market long, I'd say. It's a one-off.'

'Isn't next door identical?'

The woman shifted, fidgeting with the gold chain at her neck. 'Properties of this quality in the area are rare.'

Ginny stared and said nothing. It was her favourite way to flush someone out.

'Seventy-two hundred bond, eighteen hundred. Per week.' The woman's polyester grin returned.

'Yet grey can be so bland,' Ginny said. 'Modernism. I may as well look now I'm here.' She left the woman in search of a staircase. The last time Ginny had been here, when the site was a confusion of exposed metal rods and beams, she knew the views would mirror those of her dream block on the other side. Upstairs featured further grey. Or variations of. Thick slabs of dull, marbled tile ran behind glaring porcelain bowls. The carpets of the bedrooms were short-pile smoke, the master of which opened onto more slabs of outdoor non-slip ash. The kitchen bench stretched half the length of the house. Ginny shook her head at its steely sheen. *So boring.* She wanted to yawn. *I can't believe I was jealous. Of this.* She moved onto the balcony. Lone casuarinas dotted the borderline of the cleared grass field. *It's such a diminishment.*

Staring over the railing to the ground below, she noted the extreme sharpness of the boundary made by the carport tiles and freshy laid grass. *I'm sorry*, Ginny offered, *that this is our best. And you have to wear it.*

A couple came onto the balcony. They lingered on the railing and surveyed the park. One pointed to the winding water.

After a silence, the boyfriend spoke. 'Beautiful, isn't it?' he said turning to Ginny.

She nodded.

'Not often you see the world from here.'

Ginny thought of the steep street beside them.

'I suppose it's market price, considering,' the girlfriend added, sliding an arm around her partner's back. 'And you could wake up to this, every morning.' She leaned in for a kiss and he pecked her on the lips.

'They'll increase the rent once they secure a tenant, no doubt,' the boyfriend said, smiling at Ginny.

'Have you been doing the rounds too?' the girlfriend asked.

'Not really,' Ginny replied.

'I guess you're paying for the location,' the boyfriend added, looking around.

'That's the best part about it.' Ginny looked to the apartment block again. A pang of sadness shot into her back. 'Best of luck with it all.' She pushed away from the balustrade.

'You too,' they called as she went inside and walked down the stairs.

Ginny checked the backyard was clear. She walked down the four midnight grey steps and stepped onto the lawn. The sharp, square lawn was bordered by a bed of black pebbles. Tufts of ornamental grasses dotted the edging. A juvenile magnolia stood, assisted, in the far corner. Ginny dug into her pocket and whipped out the poem. She poured water from her drink bottle onto its underside, making sure to soak the turpentine seeds embedded in it. When the sheet was soggy and drooping, she scraped at the pebbles. Hitting dirt, she created a place for the poem.

Dreaming-continuous

Blue Gum grasps bitumen of slowly warming sidewalk.
Butcher bird rattles. Crow clunks — weekend replacements
for the all stations to Revesby.
Creek snores, slumped upon sandstone mattress,
enveloped in doona of fog.
Roofs peak then disappear in gully's shroud.
Spider web droops heavy with overnight kisses. Bats silent,
curtains drawn. Dog barks from Earlwood hills.
Humans will soon rise. Disrupt. We exit house.
Descend front steps, walk beneath the Blue Gum.

Sun leans a Saturday angle. I copy, shoulders touch.

Weighted we stroll

past neighbour then neighbour then almost neighbour.

Eventually stranger.

I reach for your hand because I am awake. Warm and finally

living.

Car pumps distorted rhythms down side street.

You take it. I am held.

Deep within the foundations of you.

ginny dilboong

After a second quick sprinkle, she replaced the stones until no paper could be seen from above.

'Can I help you, Miss?' the real estate woman said, clipping down the steps and into the yard.

'No thanks, I'm fine,' Ginny said, grabbing her shoelace and pretending to tie.

'Will you be putting in an application?'

'Nah,' she said standing.

'If you would like to leave your details, I can let you know if anything more suitable comes up.'

'No thanks,' Ginny said, leaving the woman.

As she exited, she turned to look at the neighbouring house. A young man was placing a real estate sign out front. Ginny noted the same blocked concrete, the same grey tiles. The same black framed windows and slate bricks.

'Copy, paste,' she said, shaking her head.

Ginny moved to the foot of the street and swung her arms in large circles, then jumped three times. Then, with a pump of her arms, she ran up the hill.

26.

I thought tomorrow would take forever to start. But it came around pretty quick, and I was pleased when Boy Scar jumped straight to it. Our first lesson was the dos and don'ts of falling. He said knowing how to fall would be really important because I'd be doing a lot of it as a girl and a baby all at once.

'The most important thing about a good fall, Spit,' he told me, 'is to make it look as if you mean it.'

'Okay,' I replied.

'Like this.' Boy Scar stretched his arms in front of him, then after a couple of quick prances, tucked his head in, rounded his shoulders and dived into the space before us. Curled into a perfect scar ball, he bounced a couple of times, then sprung to his feet, fingertips pointing to the sky. It didn't look like falling to me.

'Your turn, Sprite,' he said. 'Exactly the way I just showed you.'

While I was still thinking about pointed toes and outstretched arms, he shoved me in the back. Hard. My neck snapped back, and I crashed into Mum's lining. I could feel heat flare inside my unformed knees and palms.

'Tuck the head,' he barked. Then he grabbed me by my shoulder and dragged me to my feet. He slowly stroked some ungrown hair behind my ear. That stopped me from saying anything rude to him.

'Okay, try again. And remember … shoulders,' he said, slapping the growing places of my shoulder blades hard.

I braced for another shove. But this time he hooked his leg around my ankle and swept my feet from under me. Even though I was in no way ready, I managed to fall in slow motion. It gave me enough time to make myself into a tuck. I let my weight twirl me onto my back and the movement rock me onto my other side. With my last bit of spin, I flicked myself up onto both feet. I finished with my straight grown arms above my head, then did a loud clap. I looked to Boy Scar. His eyes were pretty wide.

'Not … bad. Not too bad at all,' he said, beginning to shake his hips with excitement. 'Let's go again.'

What followed was a series of throws, shoves, pushes and trips. Each had me somersaulting myself into some kind of ball. And every time I managed to finish upright. Once I got good at it, I made sure to end each tumble with a different decoration, a clap here or a point there. I chucked in some shimmies and flounces, hoping to impress Boy Scar. He sort of smiled a couple of times. Not huge stretchy ones. Just little curves in his lip corners.

But all that falling was for sure when my shoulders came in. All the tumbling told my body to make space for them. I also learned about the shape of my outside then too. Or at least what it would grow to be in time. All its pointy bits and softer parts. The tough and the tender spots. The diving and falling was helping me feel it all.

I was holding a squat with my fingers twinkling at my sides when Boy Scar announced, 'Onto the next lesson then. We don't have time to waste.'

'Can we have a little break?'

'What's that?' He jerked. Boy Scar had somehow managed to pull himself into a column. He towered above me.

'A rest.'

'Why does someone who isn't alive need a rest?' Then straight away he added, 'Now you know how to fall, you have to learn to climb. And, for the record,' he said butting in on himself, 'don't think you've perfected the fall part. You'll still need a *lot* of practice!'

He was now broad and thick and stretching almost to the top of Mum's cave.

'The thing with climbing,' he shouted down at me, 'is you gotta have no fear. Okay then, Spit. Up ya come.'

I looked at the tree he made himself into. Stretched tall like that, his scar seemed slippery.

'Don't have all day, Splat. C'mon, get to it!'

'How?' I yelled back.

I knew he was shaking his head cause I heard leaves swooshing somehow.

'The vine. Hurry up!'

He was getting tetchy, so instead of telling him I couldn't see a vine, and even if I could, I wouldn't know what to do with it, I reached out and put my pretend hands on his trunk. I ran them around the outside of his scratchy skin. As my arms widened around his waist, I felt a coil. It was thick, but floppy and movable.

'Finally,' he moaned. 'Now climb!'

I looped the coil in a spiral, using my almost hands to train it round his trunk. Then I hoisted a foot that I didn't really have yet onto the lowest coil and stepped onto it. I did the whole thing again. And again. And again. After the first few times it got harder. The coil was heavier, and my muscles were tireder. Even though they weren't really there. I was doing a lot of new stuff with parts I didn't quite have. But I had to keep going. There was nothing else I could do apart from twist then step then hold then repeat it all again. I thought I was a long way from the bottom, but I realised it wasn't far at all when Boy Scar shook himself really roughly. I managed to keep hold. When he stopped, I kept going. Twist then step then hold. Then twist then step then hold.

About halfway up, the insides of my feet got achy. And I got hot water bubbles under my hand and foot bits. That made it harder to hold on. I kept climbing though. I didn't have a choice. But when Boy Scar shook himself the second time, I lost my grip. I felt myself come away from his trunk. I fell backwards.

Of course, I knew to make my fall round and shouldery. And probably because I'd done it so much, I wasn't worried about getting hurt. Even from that height. When my body slapped into Mum's ruffles, I folded myself into it then let the twist force turn me. I spun around heaps before I slowed. Then from a push up I sprung up on my feet.

'Well done, Splat!' Came the yell from way above me. 'Not splatty at all! Told you I would be an excellent teacher, didn't I?' he called down.

'Ye—'

'Up you come. We don't have all day,' he demanded.

'But do I have to?' I said back to him. 'I'm sore. And I've got these hot bubbles everywhere that make it hard to grip.'

All he did was shimmer his trunk. So, I had to climb back on. And up. And keep going.

He tried to shake me off a few more times, but I grit my imaginary teeth and clenched my pretend jaw and looped my stinging, weeping, nearly formed hands under the vine when he did. There was no way I was falling and starting all over again.

I was a lot slower this time but eventually I got to the top. When I did, Boy Scar made himself into a dangly rope seat. He looped under me and cradled my bum part. When I was balanced, he gave me a tiny push. My hot, sore feet swung in the squish of Mum's cave. I lowered my hands and dangled them in her sweetness too.

'You did well, Spit. I'm pretty proud of you,' he said, wafting me.

That made me smile. A lot. I rested my head on his vine. 'Climbing is hard,' I said. 'But it's worth it.' Everything felt nice then, swinging on a scar who made himself into a tree, just so he could teach me something.

'You didn't look scared.'

'Don't think I was,' I told him. 'I just wanted to get it over with. It's been a big day,' I added softly, but he didn't hear that part.

I tilted my head back and saw that Cold Scar was directly above us.

'Look,' I said, excitedly. 'We're right near her.' I raised myself and stood on the vine swing. Then I reached up to touch her. My fingertips brushed her coldness. 'Boost me up a bit,' I said to him. 'I want to say a proper hello.'

He lifted me. My palm met hers. Her coldness felt good on my tired hand. It took away any angriness that had overtaken my skin. I spread out my fingers, tracing her graze.

'Hello,' I called to her. 'We've come to say ...' I baulked. 'Ahh, we've come to say — we love you.' I turned to Boy Scar. 'That's right isn't it?' I checked, whispering.

I heard Boy Scar sniffling and trying to hide a cry.

'And I've had the best day,' I kept going. 'Falling and climbing and tumbling around and stuff,' I said. 'And it's all because of ... my teacher. He knows a heap of stuff,' I told her. 'He's showing me things I need to know to come out a good girl baby. He's pretty cool,' I added. 'But you probably already know all about that.'

He went slack then.

Boy Scar started to shrink himself down. I could feel him holding me as we drooped. In the blink of a fully made eye, we had shrivelled back to the bottom of Mum's cave.

'Did I say something wrong?' I tucked myself between a mum fold and scar edge. 'I'm sorry if I did.'

He was quiet for a long time.

After an age, he spoke. 'Before you, I was so full of other things I didn't pay any attention to her. I'm ashamed to say it, Spit. If she knew anything about me, it was that I didn't care enough to know anything of her.'

Just then I felt sad. I wished I was sitting next to Cold Scar and I was holding her hand. His too.

'I hardly cared a thing for her when we lived. Why would she care about me now?' Boy Scar's voice was low.

'But she does! I know. She told me as much.'

I could tell he was surprised cause his scar tensed up.

'I spoke to her when I first came here,' I said. I didn't tell him she was only a dream echo and not really there. He mightn't have believed me if he knew that.

'Well, I'm glad of it. I was a poor brother to her, Sprite. Your conversation is the proof. She hasn't spoken to me at all since ...' he paused. 'Since forever.'

'But you're a great one to me!' I blurted. 'And now she can see that and feel it too,' I said. My inside beeps were fast. They thudded hard.

He puffed a laugh through his nostrils. If I had a chin, I knew he would have held it in his hands. 'If you think so, then maybe. I hope for my sake it can be true.' He sighed.

I thought then he must have been a scar for a really long time. It would also be pretty tiring being scrunched up and hard and scratchy for so long. I made myself into a soft splat and spread myself across him as much as I could.

He cradled my back. 'Maybe if you see her again somewhere, you can give her hair a quick pull from me? Just so she knows I miss her and still lo—'

'No,' I groaned. 'She wouldn't like that at all.'

'Well, flick her ear then. I know she loves that.' I felt him jiggle me, trying to shake our heaviness away. 'You have to promise you'll at least pinch her cheek and say it's from me. She won't believe we ever met if you don't do that.'

Then he started tickling me and kept at it until I lost breath through all the giggling. When I got my gulps back, I looked at him. No way could I tell him she said I'd never see her again.

'I'll do it, brother,' I told him. 'If you want me to.'

'Good, now I want to get some rest. We've got another big day tomorrow.'

I got really floaty then. Before I drifted into the I-don't-know-where, I heard Boy Scar whisper a hidden 'thank you' and a soft 'goodnight' into the unfolding darkness of Mum's cave.

27.

Inside Mum's cave, next to Boy Scar, things felt like they were moving fast, although we weren't going anywhere at all. I was getting rounder and stronger. My inside beeps were definitely more poundy. Though I didn't know if I looked any different.

Sharp bursts of huffing and a string of quick breathy *haa's* filled Mum's belly cave. I spun around to see what all the fuss was about.

'You're not going to like me much today, Spit. *Shaa*,' Boy Scar said through exhaled puffs that he timed with punches to the air.

'Who says I did in the first place?' I teased.

'Think quick,' he shouted, then threw a jab straight at my nose.

I dodged it by doing a squat then springing back straight after.

'Hmm,' he said. 'Your reflexes might be coming in early!'
I got all fuzzy when he said that. I liked making him proud.

'What are reflexes?' I asked.

'The trigger bits that make a fighter great.'

'Oh,' I said. 'Then I don't probably need them. I won't
be fighting,' I told him.

He did a huge belly laugh then. It jiggled me all over
cause I was still leaning on him. Then he did a heap of
little fist flurries. 'That's a good one, Splat,' he said between
whisks. 'Won't be fighting? You've done nothing but fight
with me since you got here. *Whaa, whaa, whaa, whaa, boom.*'

I giggled. He was right, I guess.

'Anyway, little sis, *hee, hee, haa,*' he added between air
jabs, 'your temper will come in handy today.' He curled
a slow motion hook into my side soft, stopping before
connecting. Then he swung around and did the same to
my other side. 'I'm gunna teach you how to fight, *pow,
pow, boom.* With these.' He held his clenched fists right in
front of my face space.

'But why?'

'So no one will ever have it over you.' He slapped the
back of my head with his hand.

'Ouch,' I cried. 'That hurt. Also, it doesn't make sense.'

'What? This?' He slapped me again, this time on my calf
meat. It stung.

'You better stop it,' I warned.

'Or what?'

'Or …' I knew what he was doing. But all his bouncing up and down on the spot with his silly fists bobbling everywhere was really annoying. Plus, my leg really, really hurt.

'Or this!' I stamped as hard as I could on his foot. He stopped bouncing straight away, pretty much.

'Aww,' he screamed. 'What the heck, Spit?' He doubled over and started rubbing his foot pretty hard. His face was all crinkled in the middle. I watched him take a few deep breaths. Then he looked at me. Really. Slowly. He started to walk towards me.

'When approaching your enemy …' he slow-motion talked as he moved. 'Come at them side on. Walk with your shoulder first. Stick it up near your jaw.' He thrust out his hand and tapped me on my cheek. I started retreating. 'That way you cover your squidgy bits while being half a target.' He tapped my other cheek with his other hand. 'Cause you're side on and all tightened up, *baa, baa.*' He let fly two quick slaps on the sides of my skull.

'Stop, please,' I whinged at him.

He kept on walking. So, I kept backing away.

'Is this your plan?' he said mocking me. 'With any bully or scary one coming after you?' he said, slapping at my arm. '*Please, don't be nasty to me,*' he whined, swatting my forehead. '*I don't like fighting. Waa waa waa,*' he grizzle-teased right in my face.

I looked down to check where his toes were.

'Oh no you don't,' Boy Scar said before jumping away and socking me in the ear. 'Keep your eyes up. Always,' he added, clipping my shoulder and running a slap onto my cheek. 'Never look down. Never look away.' He thrust his fist at my jaw. I tightened and hunched into a ball.

'Nope,' Boy Scar said, slapping a heap of open hand punches all over my body. 'Once you bunker down, Sprite, it's all over. You have to attack,' he said, still slapping. 'Be the aggressor. Get angry, Spit. Otherwise, you're dead meat. Do you hear what I'm telling you?'

I stayed hunched while he slapped and pushed and roughed me around.

'C'mon you silly little girl. You good for nothing jellyfish. You dumb splat that doesn't know a thing.' Some of his slaps had become punches now. And they kept pressing into me even after the hit disappeared.

I felt my heat rising. My gulps got faster.

'You're nothing but a baby that's come too late for everything,' he said. His voice was squeaky and nasty, and I hated it just then. 'Sister doesn't want you and I don't want you.' The punches were deeper now. 'And Mum hasn't even decided if you're worth the trouble yet. You're not even attached to her. She most likely knows you'll only be a weakling, destined to embarrass us all.'

Some sort of anger juice that was swirling in my gullet rushed up and flooded my mouth. It was tangy and yuck and the first thing I ever tasted. It made me go dark but calm. I felt it rush into my arm parts. It clenched my fingers. The idea of bones arrived.

I cocked back my fist, and the bile pushed it forward. I imagined what knuckles would feel like whacking into a jaw. I swung. And swung. And thrust and hurled and jabbed and hooked and cut. I started pacing as I swung. Each of my out-effort puffs was met by his sucked-in gasps. Inside waters flooded my surface and seeped through me into Mum's cave. I felt my skin tingle without having any. I'm not sure where my mind went. The force that rose inside me blacked out everything. I must have gone to a different part of me I didn't know yet, cause even though my body was doing things, my mind didn't know anything about it.

It wasn't until Boy Scar started yelling at me that my bits came back together.

'Open your eyes, Spit,' he shouted between blows. 'You need to look at what you're doing. It's important.'

I didn't want to see what a fist on meat looked like. It felt yucky enough as it was.

'Look at me, Spit. It's the only way this will stop.'

I opened one unmade eye. I saw my hand connecting with a tough chip of bone then a googly squidge of cheek.

I dropped my hands and opened both eyes. Boy Scar's face was bunged up. 'Why did you make me do that?' I screamed at him.

'You had to, Splat. I'm sorry.'

'I hate your dumb lessons,' I shouted.

'You gotta grow ugly parts of yourself too, Spit.'

'Shut up,' I said. 'You're ugly. Now leave me alone.' I had to turn away from his mashed-up face. It was making me feel sick. I gathered myself as much as I could and squiggled mostly into Mum's folds. I tried not to touch Boy Scar but bits of me still overflowed onto him. He found my hot fists and held them. His steady firmness made them feel not so sore. But I wasn't letting on.

'I don't feel anything, Spit. I'm already a scar,' he told me. 'You don't have to worry about hurting me.'

'I wasn't,' I said. 'Now leave me alone.' I turned from him. I could still feel him cradling my hands, though. Holding them like they were the most delicate things that ever existed. But I knew they were really only body mashers that loved to drip with blood. Mincing plates taking the space where girl hands should grow.

28.

How to Woman

Ginny pulled her favourite beanie down as far as she could. It didn't quite reach the bottom of her ear lobes, but she liked the shape her two high buns made within it, so she decided she could deal.

Moving from bathroom to lounge, she swept up her scarf from the armchair. And looped it round her neck. She wasn't expecting to be there long, but she knew how cold it could get at the oval, especially when the sun was obstructed by the new high-density flats. In any case, she was going early. She'd be finished by the Under Sixes' half-time.

She grabbed an almost empty plastic bottle from the kitchen windowsill. She held it up and shook. The swill of yellow-brown water bounced around and settled. *Just enough*, she reckoned, before shoving it in her backpack side pocket.

Ginny found a parking space in a quiet side street and squeezed in. She purposely steered clear of the carpark. She didn't want to take any chances of bumping into any of Nath's teammates. After parking, she made her way to the hole in the fence and scrambled through. Inside, she had a clear view of the ground – its waist-high white fence and its tired, blue grandstand. Steam from an urn rose from the canteen opposite, and even though it was only nine-forty, she could already smell split sausages oozing onto the hot plate.

On the boundary, clusters of parents chatted on the grass, sipping from lids of takeaway coffee cups. She scoffed at the caffeinated sideline. Without fail they would dedicate their earliest winter weekend mornings to cheering their children on in the greatest game of all, no matter how windy or wet or cold it was, but they would never, under any circumstances, stoop to drinking the three-dollar instant swill that exited the canteen. Even if it meant they were late for the game. The image of scuz on the lukewarm surface made Ginny shiver, and she promised herself a large mocha from the cafe on the corner before she went back to the car.

Ginny dug her hands into her pockets as she passed the uprights. Two boys were tossing balls over the crossbar. A woman paced the sideline, her voice coarse and piercing, as she screeched instructions at the little ones on the field. Her cries cannoned off the grandstand and filled the empty oval. Ginny walked towards the stunted fig, set back from the thirty-metre line. The ref's whistle sounded, and kids sprinted from the field into huddles of clapping parents.

Ginny circled the oval, following the sweeping metal fence that hemmed the sideline. She soon came to the tree. An elderly couple sat in expensive camp chairs in its shade. The lady was pouring hot liquid into the lid of a thermos held by the gent. Ginny lowered her head and kept moving. Grass thinned towards the base of the tree, and she tiptoed through the bare, patched ground and raised roots. She had every intention of speeding past it, since she was keen to get the job over and done with before any of the senior teams arrived. The last thing she wanted was to see anyone who knew him. But something about the tree made her approach its trunk and spread her palm across it.

She stood there breathing with it. A descending plane soared low overhead. The referee blew her whistle and kids surged back onto the field. A smattering of coins hit a tin cash box. A kid's nylon boot connected with the rubber of a footy. The tree told Ginny it didn't go much on rugby league either and it wished the flats didn't block the sunlight from hitting its roots all the time and thanks for stopping and speaking for a moment. The fig also said it would be nice to have a little sister growing out of a poem on the other side of the park and he'd take her by the roots under the field and would help grow her and not to worry. He'd teach her of more delicate things in life besides scrums and knock-ons and spear tackles. He also told Ginny she should wet the poem under his boughs because he was related to the creek water she carried, and it would be a wonderful thing to kiss his cousin after so long. Ginny removed her hand and took out the loose paper. Turning her back from the slouched, camp-chair couple, she doused it. Water splashed onto the ground, slapping the dirt between the fig's roots. The tree bristled as it embraced its relative.

'Oi,' shouted the old codger. He strained as he cranked his neck to look at Ginny. 'That's enough of that.'

'Disgraceful! Yes, tell her Reg,' the old bird tutted. 'There's a toilet block over there.' She raised a walking stick, pointing to the grandstand opposite.

'Wasn't gunna make it,' Ginny quipped, winking at the tree. She gathered her things and walked towards the oldies, her now sodden poem looking like a wet patch of toilet paper in her hand. 'But you guys know what that's like.' Ginny offered her wet, papered palm into the space between them. 'Anyway, up the Jets!' she said, flicking a wet hand towards the couple. Water curved into the air and smattered the old bird's foundation-filled wrinkles. A droplet landed on the old codger's lip.

'You disgusting bloody—'

Ginny turned and bounded away. From the corner of her eye, she could see the codger struggling to rise, unable to lever himself out of the deep camp chair. The old bird leaned towards him, a curdled, arthritic hand offering support but providing no help whatsoever.

In no time, Ginny was at the back of the grandstand. The bricks of the pavilion were painted powder blue, the ground all around its base was concrete. Players in different colour uniforms were beginning to mingle near the changerooms, so Ginny knew she had to be quick. Senior players would be showing up soon and she didn't want to see a single soul that might remember her. Ginny walked past three teenage boys, the smell of liniment and sport drink wafting from them. Making her way along the blue brick wall, she could see a small strip of dirt at its end. She walked towards it, realising as she came closer that there was a tap and small drain clinging to the side of the grandstand. The strip of dirt led to the front of the pavilion block and the entrance to the women's toilet.

Arriving at the dirt, she swung off her backpack and crouched, scratching a hole into the ground. She picked up the wet, flat square of paper and placed it in the hole.

How to Woman

I learnt how to woman on
Cold winter nights
Hunkered in jumper and scarf
Watching heads steam
Exerting a pheromone fog that ascended into
Beams of high floodlights

I learnt how to woman on
Damp park benches
Rising cold through denim
Under colliding four-point stars
Shedding particles, sharing debris creating
Unbreakable bonds between training cones

I learnt how to woman through
Windscreen condensation
Ugg-hugged toes wriggling
To wiper rhythms
Smearing droplets from glass
And mud into sprigs and cuts

I learnt how to woman in
Languid autumn afternoons and

nardi simpson

In forty-minute, lycra taught

Halves of quadricep and pectoral flexes

In which possession and put in and bust

And touch are normalised, required behaviours

I learnt how to woman on

Your sideline

Because I knew no trainer

No strapper, no supercoach so

I played the position a dummy

Half expected and a marquee signing needed of me

Now I am learning

How to woman

Without scoring

One Try

At a

Time

ginny dilboong

Ginny filled in the hole and looked up, across the field, searching for the fig. The fig's branch waved at her from a beam of sunlight that peeked over the flats. Ginny patted the earth and, after running her fingers under the tap, cupped a small handful of water on top of the poem. Then she rose and wriggled herself straight in her overalls again. Straightening her scarf, she walked to the exit and headed into the nearby cafe where, propped by cushions, snuggled into its corner, between sips of her large mocha, she began plotting the beginning lines to a new poem, its current working title: *eternal embrace of camping chair.*

29.

I ignored Boy Scar when he came to me on the next
tomorrow. I made myself small and as still as I could
when I heard him coming. He must have got the picture.
He just started on this weird story. I didn't care so I tried
hard not to listen.

'I don't know much about girl fishing, Spit. I suppose
you'll be shown that by Mum, or some aunties or old girls
after you're born and ready. I know you'll chuck a bit of
your new baby finger into the sea at some stage. It makes
girls into expert fisherwomen and sounds sort of cool, but
I'm not sure how all that comes about. Maybe when you
find out you can fill me in?'

Ugh, he was so obvious. I lifted my shoulder and hunched
away.

He kept going. 'You'll most likely be excellent, Splat.
Mum is the best fisherwoman ever born. She knows all

the right songs to make her the best at it. She takes pride in everything to do with fishing. And her gear is her most prized possession. The last thing she does every night is see to her nets. When I was little and still with the women, I'd fall asleep to her shadow in the firelight. While she twisted line and fixed knots and polished hooks, I'd listen to her sing her special fishing song. The fire would pop, and the coals would crackle, and her notes would sing their own song inside her tune. It was beautiful watching her. Ending days like that.'

'Lucky you,' I huffed from the middle of my turned back.

There was a pause. Then he said, 'Those full, warm nights are a faded dream for me now.'

It sounded so lonesome, I turned. I could see his mind chasing the memory. Its last bits. I looked in the direction of the thought. Trying to catch hold of its tail.

'Her songs were exactly the way she was. Strong but sweet. And clear. Magic too. She mesmerised fish. Sung them onto her hooks.' He did a little snort then. 'And it wasn't just fish she hooked either.'

'Sing one for me,' I said. I reckoned he might. Just to get me on side again.

'Oh no. No, no. That's not a thing I'm supposed to know,' he returned. 'Hooks and lines and nets are lady fishing things. So are all the songs that belong to them,' he continued. 'I want to show you how us men fish.'

'But why? That's not meant for me. That's what you said. Ages ago.' I knew he only wanted to show off. If he had to, I was going to make him squirm for it.

'I'll show you the *proper* way. Mum will like it. Trust me.'

His voice squeaked with his last word. I doubled over and laughed in his face cause his talking sounded so silly. Plus, I wasn't a man, so I don't know why he thought I'd be interested. Also, I was still angry with him. And annoyed I couldn't hear Mum's fishing song.

'Men do it with spears,' he said, ignoring me. 'And whenever you've got a spear in your hand, you need to be ruthless, Spit. That's what I was showing you yesterday.'

'Showing me huh?' I said, squeezing as much laugh out as I could.

'I wanted you to know how to hurt something, so you'd be able to—'

'What? Catch a fish? This is so dumb,' I sneered at him.

'Feed yourself,' he replied. 'And others.'

He stared at me. He made his scar eyebrows tight. He was trying to look serious. Or scary maybe. I wasn't sure which.

'This is really important, Spit. If you know how to be ruthless and hurt things, you must only do it at the right time.'

I had to butt in. I couldn't help it then. 'So, what you made me do in the yesterday was right was it?' My beeps got wilder and faster as I talked. 'Because it didn't feel very right to me.' All the pulsing was making me hot. I was about to humph away, but I felt his hand on my shoulders.

'I want you to listen to your beats. Especially when you get like this,' he said calmly. 'They're your own special thing,' he told me. 'They can help with lots of stuff. If you breathe with them, they love joining in on things.' His smoothish voice helped slow me down. My inside rhythm slowed. It was then I saw the spear, its shaft appearing in my eye line, stretching out before me.

'Beats and breaths,' he said, speaking the rhythm he wanted me to copy. 'Long and deep.' He continued to breathe in my ear. In our minds' eyes, Boy Scar positioned me behind a silvery flicker, a mullet fluttering in shallow water. 'Calm. And slow. In. And out. Beat. And breath,' he said as he curled his hand around mine at the end of the spear we held together. 'Gut. Then tail.' He pointed as he spoke. 'That's our aim. Breathe in. Then out.'

The fish bobbled in the current before us. Its tail quivering, its blunt nose pointed upstream.

'Gut. Then tail. Breathe in. Then out. Breathe in. Hold. Djura!'

We flung the spear. I felt the ache of a stretch in my growing arm. I watched as the prongs pierced the middle of the creature. It thrashed and the spear wobbled.

'Put it out of its misery, Splat. Do it quick so it doesn't suffer.'

I don't know how I knew anything then. Maybe I was in a trance from the breathing and the beeps and aims and growth. But I picked up the spear and yanked the fish from its end. Then I curled my fingers into its gills and pulled its head back till I heard its bones crack. The mullet twitched a bit. Then went limp. I held it by the head and let its body dangle. Drips of blood ran down its scales.

'Perfectly done, Spit. Good job!' He sounded proud.

'Was I ruthless just then?' I asked him. Looking at him made the river and the spear dissolve. We were back in Mum's cave – just Boy Scar and me huddled together inside the echo of what we had shared.

'Yes. Compassionate too. Both go hand in hand most times,' he said. 'When it comes to lunch anyway.'

He winked at me. I smiled. I sort of couldn't help it cause I was starting to feel good again. It felt nice smiling at him.

'Can we be friends again now?' he asked, bumping me.

'Not sure if you can be friends with a brother.'

'Maybe not. Let's say truce, then.'

'What's that mean?'

'It means peace. For now.'

'Okay,' I said.

'Just as well,' he replied. 'Look at your waist.'

I looked to my middle. A red vein wrapped around me. Its path traced the outside of Boy Scar then shot straight up the side of Mum's cave. It ended in the cold, squiggly middle of Girl Scar.

'Did you do this?' I asked, staring into his scratched-up face.

'You're attached now, Spit. No getting away. Even if you wanted.'

He was right. I tried shifting a bit but was fixed to the spot.

'Thank you.' I felt my face bit twitch. Inside water tried to push out from my unformed eyes.

'Don't thank me,' he said back. 'It was Mum. You're attached to her now.'

I said it before I knew I was going to. 'And to you as well.'

He curled around me. 'Little Sprite,' he said, 'welcome to the family.'

30.
The Weight

Whenever Ginny was asked who her people were, and that was rarely, she always said, *Saltwater*. And she was Salty, corrosive sometimes. If she was asked to elaborate, which was even more rare, she would say she was *a daughter of greatness*. Ginny Dilboong loved belonging to the glorious concrete and overflowing steel of her city. It knew her and loved her in return. That's why, whenever she needed comfort or advice, she would meander along a briny waterline and fold herself into the wharves and coves and reconstructed walkways. They were the softest skin of mother's chest, father's muscular resolve. Along the water she never felt like an orphan with no one to know her or care what she was.

This morning, Ginny picked a path along the tarred walkway. It was still early and the sun only newly stirred. The only movement was from pavement-pounding joggers and the first of the morning ferries. Ginny stared into the water. It's unagitated green held angled spears of sunlight that refracted as they crashed towards the harbour floor. The gentle lap of water on the sandstone retaining wall cooed. Ginny felt her scalp jump. She invited salt into its pores.

'Lookin deadly as always, sis,' she nodded into the water.

Ginny shuffled herself into a ray of sunlight and lifted her t-shirt, letting the heat hit her belly fat. She rubbed the sunshine in. This part of the city was her big sister. Within the hour it would become the busiest part of town, when the suits and tourists and school groups arrived. Then this place would become what they needed – the holiday destination, the workplace, the celebratory lunch site. But Ginny knew the Quay had secrets. And desires. And grudges and yearnings. That was the beauty of big sisters. That's why Ginny loved going down there. The Quay, her sister, was gregarious and bold, the things people needed and expected of her.

Ginny knew she also simmered with sensuality, beamed with knowledge. She wanted to grow just like a big sister. When Ginny felt small, she always walked and yarned with her sister on her fringes. Ginny always found kindness and warm communion with her there.

A seagull sliced the sky above her. 'And you're not the only deadly one. I'm a pretty good sis too. Don't barge into your room or steal your make up or anything. You're lucky to have me as much as I am you.'

A pair of huffing runners passed her from behind. Ginny looked at their straining calves and flouncing fluoro shorts. They moved quickly, their words bouncing in the jarring rhythm of bodies hitting path.

Ginny sighed. 'Need your advice, sis.'

She spotted an ugly orange bench and slid in. The *May Gibbs* ferry reversed, jerked a turn, then passed her.

'It's not that I regret doing it. I don't feel bad. It was the right decision. I just ...' She stilled and noticed the flag at the top of the bridge, limp and unmoving. 'I keep wondering ... is it bad I could be selfish so easily? I'm worried about that. I might be a psychopath or something.'

A sweet line of brine breeze wafted to her.

'Thank you,' she said, smiling into the sea. 'You're the only one I have to talk to.' She made herself stare directly into the sunlight. She felt the sting at the back of her eyeballs. 'The truth was, I didn't want to be chained to him. Even though I have no one.' Ginny let herself picture him. The details were almost all faded by then. She could remember his stubble, and the way it tickled her fingertips when she caressed it. 'Are you disappointed? Did I let you all down? After all your sacrifice?'

The harbour continued to shine and stir. A train's brakes squeaked as it pulled into the station. An Indian myna jumped on the railing in front of Ginny and sharpened its beak on the gleaming chrome. Black smoke spewed from a revving RiverCat as it backed out, turned, and churned through the waves. Ginny looked along the walkway, past sails and towards the gates of the gardens.

Ginny licked the salt from her lips. 'I love you guys,' she said to herself. 'And thanks. For always being here for me.'

She turned and began walking, passing the train station, crossing the new tram lines, then skirting towards the park behind the freshly renovated Customs House. Here she took out a poem she had wet back at home and sealed in a zip lock bag. Ginny smiled as she took it out. It was beginning to get hot and was heavy with fresh precipitation. She went to a corner full of shade and bursting with ferns. Quickly, she dug a hole and placed the seeded poem in.

The Weight

Why, when something is taken from your insides, do you feel its weight one hundred fold? In the weightless parts of your own self; mind and soul, as if such things suddenly become muscles that tense and knot and clutch sorrow, spearing you into depths of sea, suffocating you in oceans of grief, chaining you to dusty absence, powdering memory, and the metallic tang of the very thing no longer there?

Teens in backward caps fail to care for such things. Rather,
with delicate toe touches of Van and Nike, they flip tricks,
clack wooden boards, and slap pavers – sending kick flips,
ollies and nose grinds into the salvaged, flagship anchor
moored in forever shadow amongst the Quay, rubber
grommet wheels buoyant as they glide upon the weight.

ginny dilboong

Filling the hole, she walked up to the anchor. It rested
sideways on a block of concrete, the plaque beneath
proclaiming its belonging to the fleet's flagship. Ginny
dragged her dirt-caked hands over its still, cold shank.

Standing on the station's escalator, she noticed her
fingernails were thick with dirt. Quickly, she covered them,
pulling them away so no one else could see.

31.

After fishing with Boy Scar, I got lumpier. Sort of heavier. And stuff started to lean. I had pressings and pullings happening over every part of me. Getting guts was weird. It mostly felt like an always churn. A few times it turned into a stretch that really wanted to be a tear — it felt pretty achy.

When I asked Boy Scar if it was normal to be stretched and tugged in such ways, he said it was so long since he had grown that he couldn't remember what it felt like, but because I was a girl, I would most probably cry and whinge a lot, even if it was no big deal. He said I should do a few spins cause it might shift the hurt around and make me feel a bit better, but I had a cord wrapped around me and couldn't move like I used to. He forgot about that part.

'I can't tumble anymore,' I told him. 'What else should I do? I really need to make it stop.' I winced.

'I don't know how a girl works,' he said, laughing. 'Plus, you wanted to be born.'

If I didn't feel so hurtish I would have yelled at him. Instead, I just groaned.

'C'mon, Sprite. You'll definitely need to toughen up. You haven't even started properly growing yet. You're still just mashing around.'

'Ohh,' I cried. 'Please don't say anything if you can't be kind.'

He let out a stupid giggle-squeak. 'And what about the splitting in half bit? Wait till that starts.' A pretend smile was starting to curl his words. 'Then you'll have something to complain about.'

I really started wailing then.

'All this grumbling won't do, Sprite. You're not the only one in here, remember. Shared space.' I knew his wound hands were drawing a circle around his scar site.

I pushed a sigh hard from deep within my rumbling gut-mess.

'Maybe you need a distraction. What about a lesson?' he said, way too cheerily.

'Go away.'

'An easy one, like how to make a really sharp cutting blade.'

I doubled up. Then groaned louder.

'How about making a bandicoot snare? That's always fun.'

I was sorry I was tied into him just then.

'Leave. Me. Alone,' I said.

I wanted to go quiet but couldn't cause I began sob-groaning under my breath. Boy Scar listened for a while. I was waiting for a laugh or scoff. But neither came. I kept sobbing. I guess eventually he felt sorry for me.

'Did I ever tell you about the time I fell on a green ant nest and my face puffed up?' He waited.

Still, I heaved.

'How about when I caught Uncle with seaweed on his head pretending to be a water woman? That was a good one, Sprite. Although he made me promise to never tell anyone about that.'

'Please,' I grumbled, 'I need quiet.' I tried to fold in half, but it was exactly where the hurt was coming from. I yelled.

Boy Scar made himself warmer then. I felt the glow come into me.

'Maybe if you speak it out, it might help.' He spread himself out a bit and pulled me onto his scar. If he had a shoulder, I guess I would have been resting on it. I felt him pulse warmth rays. I snuggled into them. It didn't stop all the ache, but it did feel nice. A bit better. 'Give it a try. It can't hurt any worse that it does now,' he told me.

I shifted on him a bit. Then I took a deep gulp. 'The ache's somewhere inside. It feels deep. But also near my outside too.'

He sent a steady pulse into my side parts.

'And it's crumpled. Like fold-rockings. And the folding part really, really hurts.'

'Is there anything nearby?'

'What do you mean?'

'Can you see anything? Sometimes if you can get inside the feeling, it makes you see stuff.'

My mind fluttered from the ache a bit. Then it came. 'I'm sitting in a tree,' I said.

'Its branches?'

'The rough, itchy part. But not up. It's on its side. Under me. And it's moving up and down and folding me and making me hurt. Aww,' I yelped.

He was silent for a little while. I could feel him thinking. 'What else?' he asked.

I searched for the words to match the feeling. 'There's also a yuck in my middle. Like a dizzy ick. Whenever I go up and down, so does the sick. But the ouch is different.'

'Up and down, you say?'

I couldn't answer. I was spit-swallowing and it was awful.

'On a sideways tree. I think you're fishing! That's a canoe. Mum's taken you out. Onto the harbour!'

'Well, I don't like how it feels.'

'Oh, but you will, Sprite. You will grow to love everything about it.'

Boy Scar then told me how hard it is in a canoe cause your arms do most of the work. You have to have a strong back or you'd never get to the places you're going, and your gut has to hold on to all the parts that are moving, and stay still and strong, at the same time, and that's hard work too. 'That could be what the hurting is about,' he told me.

I guess he could have been right.

Then he started going on about the tides and the swells and currents and winds and stuff, and how they were other things that needed effort to push against and pull through. Not to mention actually hauling up heavy nets and big fish on little handlines. Then there was watching your fire and looking after your bait, but those things didn't sound like they would hurt your body too much.

'There's heaps of things you need to do in a canoe, Splat,' he told me. 'That's why us men don't bother with it,' he said. 'Why muck around with all that when you can just finish em off with a spear?'

I was going to say something about feeding more than just yourself, but my ache heated up. So, I let it go.

Then Boy Scar went on about how he and his fathers always looked after the women's boats – reheating and reshaping or rebinding them up whenever they needed. He said it was his job to harvest and heat the gum for the cracks and the holes. He said he didn't mind it, but mucking around with plants was mostly women's work, so he nagged and nagged to be the bark cutter, climbing to mark out the shape of the next new canoe. I said his job basically sounded like messing around with plants as well, and he waved me around so that my sick flared up.

'Anyway,' he continued, 'I was the best climber by far. You know that for yourself, Spit, as I was an excellent teacher of it. And I probably would have been the next cutter, if things didn't go the way they did.'

I was too sick to work out what that meant. I stayed quiet. So did Boy Scar. I wondered if he had drifted off somewhere, he was silent for that long. And because it was so quiet, I got to thinking about my ache and ick and started groaning again.

The sound must have returned him. From where, I don't know.

'In a canoe,' he told me, 'Mum is at her most beautiful. And powerful. I can't wait for you to see it, Splat. Everyone else chops when the swell rises and plunges their oars as deep as they can. But Mum slices. Maybe that's what's happening to you.'

'Aww, don't,' I groaned.

'She slices the water,' he said over the top of my moaning, 'then places it where she wants. Her arms glisten and her hair bounces and her shoulders are as straight as a spear. She looks so wondrous when she glides. Within the everything. Water. Land. Sky. Air. You name it. The way she is on the water comes from somewhere special. Maybe her waters inside.'

It did sound pretty wondrous.

'She goes into her middle,' he continued. 'It's like she listens to her centre then asks her body to respond.'

'I don't get it,' I said.

'She absorbs the sea. She makes herself into it. So, she is the water around her canoe as well as the soak within it.' He could tell I wasn't following. 'Let me show you,' he said. He flattened himself. 'In ya get.' He gathered me on the centre of his scar. Then he curled a rough, ringed bow around me and told me to hold on. 'Ready?' he warned.

'Wait,' I said.

But he had already started rocking me. 'The first rule of the water, Spit, is don't overcorrect. Go with the bumps. Melt into the movement.' He started shaking and reeling me in every different direction there was. The achy dullness filled my whole bottom half now.

'Please, it hurts,' I pleaded. The jerks and circlings sent shooting pains right through me.

'Don't fight it. Absorb it, Splat, like Mum does. I know you can find a way.'

He kept shaking me. I thought I would spew with all the cold then hot flashes overtaking me. And all the gross heaviness trying to weigh me down. I tried to do what Boy Scar said and greet whatever was churning, and take it by the hand. So, instead of being all hard and closed, I let it come into me. I leaned into its swell. As soon as I did, I felt relief.

'I think something's happening,' I yelled to Boy Scar, who was still rocking and shaking me pretty hard.

'Good, Splat,' he shouted back. 'Maybe you've cracked it!' He shook me harder. I wobbled but focused on keeping myself soft inside. A word began to form. I said it to myself before shouting it into the fullness of mum's cave.

'Hips!' I cried. 'I'm doing it, brother! My hips are coming in!'

'You are, Sprite. Glide, command the water. Glorious!' He yelled. 'I can see you high in your canoe. Looking just like her. I'm watching you. Like I used to watch her. From behind a wattle shrub on the rock ledge.'

I smiled and waved up at him from the water. I had found a groove and felt balanced. 'My hips are growing. I can feel them, brother, they ride the flow.' I giggled. 'Why didn't you tell me hips were such glorious things? The levers of a body!'

I felt him shrivel. Shrink a bit. The canoe dissolved from beneath me.

I returned to his scar. 'Did I do something wrong?'

'No.' He tried a quick bounce as he spoke, but his heart wasn't in it.

'Why are you sad, then?'

'Hips are a woman's business, Sprite.'

'Don't men have them?'

'Not women's ones.'

I was confused. 'They're different?'

'Of course!' he replied. 'Ours are fixed in place, so we can run and track and climb.'

'But we do that as well, don't we?'

'Yes,' he said. 'But women's hips do other things,' he whispered.

'Like what?'

'That I can't tell you, Spit. A woman will have to show you that.' He sounded sad. And small.

'You miss them, don't you?'

'We're a good pair.' He tried to sound cheerful. 'You crying over hips and me missing ...'

'Mum? Sister?'

Boy Scar stayed still. And silent. I knew he was hiding his face from me. His thoughts as well. After a very long time, he eventually spoke. 'She's building you from the inside out, Spit.'

I felt my hips. They were hot but not achy anymore. I felt strong. That's probably why I said it. 'The way girls are supposed to be made.' I was happy that I did.

32.

Boy Scar loved all that adventurous stuff like running or pushing or throwing. He showed me how to chase roos and dive for lobsters and scoop honey out of trees. Things like that. Tiring things. Hurting things. Things that made me sore and grumpy when they were over. I grumbled a bit about them. Well, a lot actually. But they were sort of fun at the same time.

Whenever he showed me something new and I got it right, he'd turn into one huge scar smile. Or he'd do a backflip. Or sing out a big *yuwin*! I loved when he did. It was better than his teasing and barking instructions. If I could make him smile, I knew his laughs after that would be proud. Not annoying and hurtful like they sometimes could be.

Sometimes Boy Scar taught me sit-down things too. Like how to start a fire or sharpen an axe. I liked those lessons much more than the running and jumping and chucking stuff. So, the next time he told me he wanted to show me something, I really hoped it was a sit-down thing.

'Come on, Spit. Sit,' he said patting a smooth part of his scar.

I smiled and slid closer to him. 'What are we doing today?' I asked, excited.

'Patterns,' he replied.

In my mind I saw him pull some bark from a tall, red and brown tree. Then he teased it between his fingers. He did this a few times to make sure the strands were pressed tight together. Then he sucked it and dipped it into a puddle of white paint. 'Close your eyes,' he said to me.

He dragged a wet line beneath my eye to the bridge of my nose. Its coolness calmed my face. The dampness of the line soon crackled up and became dry and tight. I scrunched my nose a bit.

'Hey, don't do that,' he growled.

'It's itchy,' I said.

'You're twitching it off. Keep your face still or the pattern'll be ruined,' he said.

He did another line beneath the first one. I tried not to think about the wetness and then the dry tightness.

'Better,' he said, then did the same beneath my other eye. This time it tickled my bottom eyelashes, so I jerked a bit.

'Argh,' Boy Scar moaned. 'You mucked it up. Gotta start again,' he said, spitting on the wonky line then rubbing it off my face.

'Sorry,' I said to him. 'But it feels weird. I can feel every little stroke, even though I don't have a face.'

Boy Scar looked at me. Then he sighed. 'Maybe this might work better.' He held my soon-to-be wrist and straightened my arm in front of him. 'When you're born and growing up—'

'In the outside,' I interrupted.

'In the outside,' he said. 'You will wear your patterns, so everyone knows who you are and who you belong to.'

'Okay.'

'And our patterns tell everyone we belong to Mum.'

'Right,' I said. 'Try again,' I added. 'I'll be really still now I know all that.'

Boy Scar dipped his brush in the paint again. 'She starts in our middle,' he said, looping an arch from my chest. 'Then flows down,' he added, curving the line along my shoulder and down my forearm. 'Centred and strong. On water and on land.' He cocked his head to the side to look at his line work. Happy, he did the same to my other side.

I watched the wisp of the bark flow over my arm. As he went on painting, we both went so quiet that our beats heard each other. It felt close. And special. So special that Boy Scar spoke about things I'd never heard before. He told me as he continued with more lines that when he was born, there was a big celebration because Mum was beautiful and clever, and her family was really important. Plus, he said, he was a boy, so that made everyone happier. He said when he was a baby, he didn't like being in a canoe cause it was sometimes cold, and when the water was rough, he'd spew up and Mum would get angry. He said his favourite fish was sand whiting because it was sweet. He told me that once, before he died, he got a little bone stuck in his throat, but Mum rammed her fingers down his gullet and pulled it out.

He said he loved it when he was moved on to the men cause he could make sharp things and throw stuff and they wouldn't rouse him. But that he did miss cuddles after that sometimes. Especially at night. He made me promise never to repeat that bit. To anyone ever. He said it wasn't too bad, though, cause his legs got strong from running and chasing and tracking a lot.

Boy Scar told me there were secret songs and dances I'd never be allowed to do or hear or even think about. When I told him that didn't sound fair, he said sometimes life was like that, but I'd have secret girl things too. That made me okay with it, I guess.

He said he hated killing echidnas, even though they tasted so juicy and yum, cause they were slow and fat and couldn't defend themselves. But he loved jumping on top of great big goannas when they thrashed around and tried to poison him. Whacking one on the head and feeling its limp body swing against his back as he walked into camp was the best feeling ever, he said.

He told me he cried when he was shown his new baby sister. He made out the tears were because he was annoyed he'd have to fetch water and make fires and look out for her and stuff, but really they were because he felt happy. And proud. He said he'd been alone in Mum's insides for so long he couldn't remember what anyone looked like anymore.

Boy Scar told me he had a sweetheart. He stopped talking for a really, really long time after he mentioned her.

He told me his father got sick with sores first. Then Sister. Then Mum. Then him. He said that even though Mum was weak, she fetched water and washed the pus from their sores every day. He told me Sister died first, in the morning, and that his father died later that night. He said Mum's crying was so hollow it shooed the birds from the trees. He said they were both too weak to bury them, so Mum placed their arms around each other and covered them with bark from a Tea Tree. Then they left them. He said they stumbled to a different place, but he knew he was going to die soon too. He said Mum wiped his face until he couldn't feel it anymore, and that he was scared to die but when it happened it didn't hurt. Not like being born did.

'All this outside stuff, or your version of it anyway, is something you have to look forward to, Sprite,' he said to me. He was shiny then. And flashing.

'Why you are still here, but a scar?' I asked.

'Dunno.' He shrugged. 'I tried a lot of times to go to the outside. Willing and wishing and magicking myself away, but I can't seem to make it work.'

'Where would you go if you could?' I asked him, settled in his warm pulsing centre.

'To the time before the sickness. To my sweetheart, Mugung, and her hair.'

'She sounds beautiful,' I said. I really meant it.

'She was.'

He held my arms out for me to look at. The thinnest of white lines ran down them. My pretend muscles shimmered in Mum's cave waters. I felt a flood of something new in my insides then. I think it had something to do with the patterns being like the marker of bones to come.

33.
Always

Ginny woke up with the shits.

Her days had been moving excruciatingly slowly. Money was non-existent. Words weren't making sense anymore. She was stuck and bored and probably lonely. Even her sleep was in a funk.

This morning, she had already cried and laughed till she cried again, and it had only just gone eight-thirty. She was all over the place and knew she should probably get outside. And around some people. Little ones preferably. *Hopefully they'll fall over or chuck a tantrum or cause a scene. It'll be nice to watch someone else squirm for a while*, she thought.

She decided her day should involve a long stint at the kids' play park beside the river. *Free entertainment and fresh air guaranteed.* She launched herself out of bed and squirmed into a pair of tights swiped from the bedroom floor. She bundled her hair and manoeuvred into bra and t-shirt. 'Worth a try,' she said, grabbing her bag and stepping onto the street.

The sun was young but strengthening. It would get sticky later. 'Bring it,' she said. 'Do your worst, Big Man,' Ginny taunted, slapping beams into her shoulders.

She lowered her sunnies, smacked pawpaw cream on her lips, and started towards the park. She was up for the fight. Needed it. For sure she'd get hot. Probably burnt. Absolutely she'd start sweating. She'd totally get uncomfortable in all her tight stretchy things. But for certain there would be a breeze lifting from the water. Even if it was a warm one. That would be enough to cool her. In a couple of days, she'd proper tan up. Her spirits lifted as she walked, buoyed by the notion of a fresh coat of shimmering chocolate brown. She looked pretty deadly in a new tan. And that made her feel sexy. 'Look out world,' she yelled into the street. 'Ginny might be making a comeback.'

Ginny continued her cement descent towards the river. Barely more than glorified sludge, the waterway continued its meandering and tiding, despite centuries of modification and misuse. Its muddy bed was fetid, poisons and metals infiltrating the ooze. The fish had come back, but couldn't be eaten. Ibis and swamphens picked through plastic and styrofoam tides. Radioactive mud crabs scuttled over tyre rims and sewerage pipes and rusted shopping trolleys. Swarms of retiree volunteer bushcarers fussed on the banks, planting Dianella and Native Sarsaparilla and Pigface for designer dogs to take craps in. Developers donated their sandstone slurry for councils to commission questionable pieces of public art along the river's edge. And a breeze always lilted through the Casuarinas. The moon still massaged her waters in and out of the bay. Wattle pollen and paperbark continued to fall from branch overhangs. They kissed the water's surface, then danced with chip packets and busted balloons before sinking into the stream.

A coupling of inevitable decay, Ginny thought as she strode towards the water. *Nature. Rubbish. Each tethered to the other's fate.*

'You're a better woman than me,' she called to the current.

The playground was in a sheltered grove of mature Poplars. Scatterings of benches were arranged under a tin gazebo. Ginny walked to a deserted table, put her feet on its bench and foisted herself on its top. A kid was squirreling up the playground's climbing ropes, his pushbike collapsed against the structure's base. His dad was loitering nearby, pretending to encourage him while he scrolled on his phone.

She watched the boy. He was seven maybe. His knees got in the way a lot. They were angular and wide. He wobbled on the red rope. When the boy went to stand upright, he overbalanced. His weight flung backwards, and he struggled to hold on. Stabilising, he crouched, knees acting as ballasts. He looked at his dad to check if he would get in trouble. The father was grinning at his screen. Didn't notice a thing.

A giggling, excited family burst from the carpark and overflowed into the playground. Ginny watched as they walked towards the tables. Each member of the party carried either a bowl of food or bag of presents. Two men lugged an esky. They walked straight to the hot plates and plonked them down.

A woman approached. 'Excuse me, are you saving the table?'

Ginny marvelled at the lady's eyeliner. Its dramatic almond outline made the hazel at their centres pop. The woman's delicate gold nose ring winked in the sunshine.

'A party also?' The woman smiled.

'Oh, I'm just ... hanging out ... at the playground.' Ginny winced inside.

'Could we have this? We're expecting many. I think we'll need both.'

Ginny looked to the table next to her, already laid with platters of cut-up fruit, bowls of tabouli and mounds of triangle-cut flatbread. She jumped from the table top and slid her backpack on.

'Amira, come say thank you to the nice lady,' the woman urged. 'It's her tenth birthday today,' she added, smiling.

'Thank you,' the girl sang. 'I like your sunnies,' she said before sprinting to the roundabout, grabbing its bar, and running a furious circle before jumping on.

'Very kind. Please, take this,' the mother offered. 'It's fresh.' She held a sugar dusted biscuit in a paper serviette out to Ginny.

'That's fin—'

'No. You have to. It was made for you.'

Ginny looked at the golden pastry's spiralling cone.

'Maamoul,' the woman said, taking Ginny's hand. 'Sweet.' She smiled, placing it in Ginny's palm. 'By my mother. Mama!' she called, gesturing.

Another woman, a shrunken version of the one before her, waved at Ginny then continued pouring pistachios into a bowl. Ginny smelled the biscuit. Amira and the kids squealed as they spun on the roundabout. Women fussed and laughed as they covered the table.

'You have a beautiful family,' Ginny said, smiling.

'As do you,' the woman returned.

Ginny's chest froze. Her throat seized. She felt a tear roll from her eye.

The woman placed her palm on Ginny's cheek. 'I see their kindness in you,' she said, wiping the droplet with her thumb. The woman held Ginny's gaze. Soon, she felt warmth returning, rising from her gut and filling her chest.

'They are blessed,' the woman added, moving her hands to Ginny's shoulders.

'Mama! Mama!' called Amira across the playground. 'I am flying. Look!'

The woman turned to see her daughter waving as she pushed all her weight back then forward in a huge arch on a swing. She rose her hand to her daughter.

'And so shall you be,' she said, returning to Ginny.

'Maktub,' offered the older woman as she passed with a wad of serviettes and placed them on the bench.

'That's right, Mama, it is written,' said the woman. 'For you. By you too.' The woman nodded as she squeezed Ginny's hand.

'Thank you,' Ginny whispered.

Grinning, the woman turned and resumed fussing over the elaborate birthday spread.

Ginny went to the water and sat, wiggling her legs above the water line.

'Hi,' she began tentatively. A wind lifted off the water and whooshed through the casuarina needles, sending a wide wash of white noise into the playground. 'Thought I'd come down to cheer myself up,' she went on, 'but, of course, I'm the only loner here.' A fat silver mullet speared out of the water and side-slapped back into the depths. Ginny watched the ripples grow as they fanned across the water. 'Didn't think it through entirely. There are relatives swarming all over this joint.' She followed a puffer fish as it cruised amongst the young mangroves. 'Usually I don't care, but I'm off a bit. Don't know why.' She sighed. A bowed eucalypt curved on the other side of the water. Its trunk shone silky streaks of silver and caramel. 'I mean, I don't mind being alone. I like doing quiet, solitary, thoughtful things, but sometimes ...' Her voice faltered. 'I miss being held.' Her throat caught again. She struggled to continue. 'I have all this love. But no one to give it to.'

A boy on the flying fox squealed. Wind lifted again, rustling the leaves of the trees across the river. 'My own fault, I guess.' She looked into the branches of the She Oak. They were long and dead straight. Probably would have made great spears, back in the day. 'I am grateful,' she continued. 'You've made a place for me here, inside your greatness. That's deadly.' Another fish jumped, splashing an oyster growth in the mud beneath her feet. 'But, no offence, it's cause you are so endless, so great an expanse that I feel so ... insignificant. Forgotten.'

She felt her eyes begin to swell again. Something told her that crying was good cause it was proof she was related to the river. And in that way her family was there and holding her all the time. *It lives inside you. As you do it. As it carries you. Always.* That made the tears flow more. She cried silently beside the river as a toddler in the park behind her stacked it then wailed. Eventually, Ginny pulled herself together, wiping her dripping nose on the shoulder of her shirt. She flicked the remaining mucus into the water. A long-necked turtle, tasting it, blew two bubbles of thanks out her nostrils. 'As long as you know me, and have my back,' she added, 'I'll be fine.'

Ginny jumped to her feet and turned, facing the playground. People were everywhere. She set off along the walkway, following the river's curve. Crossing the bridge of a modest gully, Ginny left the path and traipsed into the undergrowth. Pulling up before the water she bent and brushed at the leaf litter and fallen bark. Creating a patch, she dug a hole then pulled out her poem. She rifled in her bag. 'Shit,' she spat, realising she had left the filled water bottle on the kitchen sink. 'Oh well,' she said, wiping the paper against her wet underarms. 'In the spirit of grey-water recycling and that kind of stuff.' After rolling it around a bit, she removing the paper. She sniffed it. 'Phew-ee! Potent. Guess that's a good thing.' She placed the poem in the hole. 'Probably only in this instance,' she added, covering it up with soil and leaves.

Father MyMother Water MyEarth

The sand is orange in your triangle low tide

Where severed strands of seaweed roll in

Waterlogged outbreath of current

Wet lickings of hairs on your big toe

Your eventual eviction to the right water's

Wrong edge, every detail of

New world unrest uneasy

Everything – upside down

The waterline is devoid of curve and softness

On your cruel, lashed stone shore

Cuts from core and developer soaked

Edging pour concrete upon your fierceness

Encasing you in enemy shoal

New worlds riches drown

Everything – upside down

ginny dilboong

Still crouched, Ginny noticed a large, spindly mosquito sucking her forearm. She watched as its stomach swelled and began pulsing in time with her own heartbeat. Allowing it to finish, she watched it fly off and dissolve into the mangroves. Ginny was well past the park and on her way home when, downstream, a Magpie swooped and swallowed the mosquito whole.

34.

When I began splitting in half, I couldn't do anything but cry. And sob. And weep. Boy Scar gave up trying to get me to learn things while I was like that. Couldn't stand all the whingeing, he said. But I couldn't help it. I half expected him to dissolve from me or go away forever. He didn't. He just let me toss and squirm around on him. He sometimes sent warmth into my never-ending aches. I was grateful for that. But I didn't thank him. I couldn't do anything but twist in knots and bawl and sniffle and stuff. I was happy he was there and helping a bit and not bossing me about when I was in pain and tearing.

The only good part was that Boy Scar had nothing other to do than talk. He did it, he said, to drown out all my woefulness. He said all my shifting and squiggling around was one thing, but the non-stop howling was another.

'If I gotta listen to something, Spit, it's not going to be your blubbering,' he said. 'Plus, I'm a pretty fantastic storyteller, if you haven't already noticed. So,' he went on, 'my voice will be just the thing. It'll be good for you to have something else to focus on,' he added. 'Will be for me, at least.'

So, he started telling me about his friends. And all the silly things they said and did to each other most days. The hidings they got. Or watched. Or dodged. Or got for others. The jokes they made. The tricks they pulled. The near-death escapes and close shaves they got in and out of. All the things they killed or saved or broke or made. All the running away. And chasing. And all the ribbing.

'What's that?' I asked through pangs and sharpness.

'Ribs are bones,' he told me. 'When you poke them, they hurt like nothing else. But they're ticklish sometimes too,' he said. 'Ribbing is what boy – what men do, Spit,' he said. 'It's an art. A manly one. Basically, a hurtful laugh … or a funny cry. Girls wouldn't get it.'

'Ribs?' I asked.

'No, the craft of it all,' he replied, swankily.

I felt a hurty lean under my beep. 'I think maybe I'm getting them,' I told him.

'Probably,' he said. 'My stories are pretty powerful like that.'

He kept on. All the names the friends had for each other. The words they used to make each other cry. And the laughs they had at the snot and the tears that streamed afterwards. Also, all the legendary farts and unforgettable cheap shots and stinking gut burps. He told me about all the naughty stuff they did. And the brave stuff too. And a lot of other things that made no sense at all. If I was my normal self and not breaking in two all the time, I might have told him boys seem to goof around a lot. And do what they pleased too much. But I kept the thought inside to split and separate with everything else.

Then he spoke about the men. Each one had something out of whack, he said. Crooked elbows, wonky eyes, stumpy legs and wrong way fingers. Squeaky or whistly or stuttery or dumb sounding voices. There were shrivelled chests and fat hips and big and small and odd size balls. Boy Scar laughed hard when he spoke about that. I didn't get it, so I just stayed quiet. He told me of all the cranky ones and lying ones and kind ones. His favourites were the ones that could watch anyone and imitate them perfectly, down to the way they sat or spoke or walked or sucked their teeth.

'They are the cleverest, Sprite. Funny and smart and always watching. You can't get anything over them,' he said, glistening. 'And what you don't want to do is anything foolish in front of them. They'll never, ever let you forget it.'

Men also seemed to have sayings they loved repeating all the time. Boy Scar told me about all the 'don't make me get ups' and 'I'll give you something to cry abouts' and the 'all mouth no ears' men. The 'speak ups', the 'just let me do its' and the 'little shit eaters'. Their memories made him laugh hard. Then there was all the 'hurry ups' and 'sit downs' and 'go aways' and 'be stills'.

'Sounds like you,' I said to him. It slipped out. I was still in pain. I wasn't really thinking about what I was saying. I held my beeps, waiting for him to rouse.

He just did a soft huff instead. 'Thank you, Splat,' he said to me. Then grinned and rippled warm pulses into my back.

He told me about even more men with scars all over them. Marks that lit up shoulder muscles and drew out chest bones. Back-pattern cuts and side-scrape lines and leg notches that made their bodies shine when they rubbed themselves with fish fat. Or walked out of the water. Those scars were different to the regular type, he said. From the gashes and wounds you'd see on thighs and shoulders and foreheads. From fights. 'Those scars,' he said, 'the everyday ones are usually to do with some female mischief.'

'That's what you are, hey,' I told him.
'What?'
'A scar over a woman. You're more wound than marking.'

Boy Scar went really quiet then. And his heat didn't turn off exactly, but it spread out and went low, so it felt like it wasn't even around anymore.

'Sorry,' I said in a little voice. 'I didn't mean to upset you.' If I could, I would have thrown my arms around Boy Scar's neck right then. Mum's cave went so still I heard our beeps whooshing in time with each other again. I could tell they were listening too, waiting to hear how he would reply.

'It was night,' he whispered. 'So, the first time we met, I didn't even see her.' He jiggled me around. I got comfortable on him and squirmed down a bit.

'Lucky. If I would have made her out, I would have for sure chucked a spear straight at her. If I had pelted my spear, Splat, that would have been the end of it. Over before it even started,' he said.

'What are you talking about?'

'Her hair.'

'Whose?'

He warmed again. I felt it.

'Hers, of course, Mugung. My possum sweetheart. She's got good hearing, so she heard me draw it back and aim. "Yokai," she yelled. "Who's there?" Well, I thought it was my dinner shouting at me, so I jumped. Kicked my toe on a dumb fig tree root. "Keep your distance, you evil creature, or I'll put this spear right between your eyes." I tried to sound brave, but I won't lie, Spit, deep down I was trembling. A talking possum is a scary thought. Especially at night. Plus, now I had a sore toe, and I wasn't thinking straight.'

'I know what you mean,' I said.

'And then I heard, "Who dares challenge me?" It sounded nasty. I hid behind the tree trunk a bit, just in case it was going to jump out and scratch me to pieces. Then a rustle in the bush sent me scurrying into the fig's branches. A terrible rumbling growl followed it. I hid in a crook as the growling got closer. It came right up to me, Splat. Then that possum launched itself. I yelped and slipped from my hiding spot between the branches. I looked upon my tormentor as the moonlight made it out. The talking, growling devil possum was a girl. Or I should say a woman, Splat, for that's what she was. Slender and magical and glorious. With wide, dark eyes and long arms. Her hair was bundled. Wound on the crown of her head in a heap. The string that bound it, fur. "Who's the possum now? All frightened and big-eyed and huddled up a tree?" she said. That was the first time I saw her. After that, she was all I ever saw.'

Boy Scar pulled me into him. I flinched cause I was still churning.

'We used to sneak to each other most nights. I asked her to wear her hair down so no one would see us. I was also worried some silly boy would make the same mistake I nearly did and spear her. But she refused. She said she liked wearing her hair that way. It made her feel beautiful, and she wouldn't change it for anyone. So, I set to trying to swear everyone off possum meat. Spit,' he said, 'each time she smiled it was like the sun and the stars and the waves exploding inside me all at once.'

'Sounds painful,' I told him.

He laughed, then bounced me on his scratchy scar lap a couple of times. 'Growing with someone does hurt. Because it is so beautiful.'

I thought about it a bit. 'Well, I think I hate it,' I said, but only quietly.

'Being made by others is magnificent, Sprite. Trust me. Honour the hurt. It is making you who you are.'

Just then, Boy Scar shifted colour, turning from pink to grey. I panicked cause he seemed to be draining away from me. I tried to spread myself across him. He began to shrivel, his scar contracting.

'What's happening?' I cried. 'Are you unwell?'

We looked down to see white veins rush and overtake his reddish middle.

'Dearest Spit,' he said to me, deflating.

'Where are you going?' I yelled. My insides were burning.

His warmth surrounded me. 'You were what I needed. Not the other way around.'

'You're leaving?' I sobbed into his growing coldness.

'Be brave, Splat,' he called as he faded from Mum's inside. 'Try not to forget me when you are born and in the outside,' he yelled just before he disappeared.

I watched as the memory of his claws retracted. His fringes puckered and his scar dissolved from under me. All that was left in Mum's cave was me. And the cord that bound me into her folds.

35.

Blister Pack

Ginny waited till nightfall. It would most likely be busier than any other time. The local weirdos loved to do things like go to the cemetery at night. And put on gigs or chuck parties amongst the rows of lost souls. Walking home a couple of weeks ago, she had clocked a birthday in full swing at eleven pm. The glow sticks caught her eye. They illuminated the taut, helium numbers — three and zero. The revellers had repurposed a sinking grave slab as a party table. Ginny looked at the tilted champagne bottles and dishes of marinated mixed olives as she passed, recoiling at the sacrilege. Then she kept walking. She figured the dearly departed, seeing as they had already assumed the position, deserved to enjoy the perks of kicking up their heels.

On this night, she was certain there'd be people there. But hopefully they'd be too occupied, too stoned, too lovey-dovey or too tipsy to care about her creeping around. She needed the cover of nightfall to make her brave enough for what needed to be done.

The graveyard was shrouded in darkness despite being in the middle of a busy suburb. Its only illumination came from a high sensor light bolted to the corner of the adjoining sandstone church. The rest of the surrounds were poorly lit. Remembering her promise to be sparing with her phone, she left it in her jacket pocket while she waited for her eyes to adjust. She could hear clusters of murmuring voices scattered throughout the cemetery and a clump of mature bamboo that sprouted from the middle of the burial ground creaked in the gentle air that flowed amongst the headstones. Once Ginny had made out the irregular rows, she began walking. She followed the trail of large monuments. The graves of rich, landowning types from the early days of the colony provided the perfect wayfinding to the grave she had selected. Most of the information on these fine epitaphs was painted gold. It was clear to Ginny that their families believed only incredibly heavy obelisks or sad-eyed, marble angels could do justice to the importance of their loved ones' days.

Scattered between these monuments were graves of regular people. Smaller lives, smaller memorials. Oval and arch stones with capitalised names and obligatory numbers. At the rusted, wrought iron grave of Hubert Henry Garfield Snr, Ginny slowed. It was only a handful of steps from there. she bent low to the ground, searching the shadows for the quarter sandstone slab lying flush with the ground. A flirty titter drifted from a couple canoodling a few rows away. Ginny focused on the worn grass path before her, hoping to avoid any living-couple kink. Moonlight shone on the fallen stone. She stopped then crouched. She mouthed the words illuminated before her. 'Our Dearly Beloved Daughter, taken from us too—'

Ginny flung her backpack on the ground and rifled through it for her notebook. She took out the red pad and pulled its elastic from the front cover. Then, using the ribbon, she opened to the page with the loose sheet tucked into its spine. Ginny held the paper up against the dark sky. The soft, silver gleam caught the seeds embedded in the paper. The round, Red Gum pips appeared like scales in the moonlight. Ginny read aloud the beginning words of a line overlayed on the seeded, recycled paper.

She let the weight of the phrase's tail echo and hit the far wall. Ginny whisked the paper out of the light and yanked out a water bottle that was rammed into the side pocket of her backpack. Making sure she didn't spill any on the fallen, fractured headstone, she soaked the paper and folded it into a tender, small square. As she brought it to her lips and kissed it, a draught travelled across the bone yard. Squatting in her favourite skirt beside the baby's grave, the wind reminded her she wore no underwear.

She scratched out a hole beneath the stone just big enough to work half the paper into. Manoeuvring it into the slot she created, Ginny covered the rest of the poem with thick, black dirt. After patting it down, she topped it with a small soaking. As the water lowered itself in moonlight, Ginny felt her heart pound hard in her head. The rhythm of its pulsing filled her ears, and she became dizzy. Falling to her bottom she reclined next to her freshly buried seeds. As she closed her eyes, tears pooled in the wet dirt.

Blister Pack

It hides in an earring bag, amongst silver rings, woven pink
spirals and the gold dangles I wore that night. Metallic
stop-and-go backing dissolves into other trinkets. Unzipping
the pink faux leather, the hoard tinkles, winks. I notice
only the buckled tab – the shrivelled shell I cycled around.
The blister pack is crammed into a purse of most intimate
possessions – finishing touches I use to entice another's.

I take it out. Half the pills in popped plastic remain.
I turn it over, caressed days falling through fingers, out
of reaching hands. Swallow yellow, for coiled, coupling,
pressing against you. Released white, a single embrace
of pillow, water bottle. Agreed flow. Punctured bubbles
smell our sex suspended. Legs mid-air. Impregnating
heat and friction. When I was using, I said you only
live once. You said we nearly didn't live at all.

The unfinished blister pack screams life unlived. Cycle
aborted; breathless life thwarted. Holding onto half of what
almost was soothes, for now. I'll keep it in my earring bag,
buried in cheap jewels, and blurred, messy nights. I will
wonder what the untaken might have been. How love filled
the hours. Half days rolling in sheets of living and life. I yearn
for a pill to tell me what life will come. Rather than show
parts that have died.

ginny dilboong

She was roused by a light shake of her shoulder. A man
crouched beside her, his blue-grey eyes worried.

'Miss, miss,' he said. 'Are you okay? Do you need help?'

Ginny pushed herself from the ground.

'Did you faint? Maybe you should have some water.' He twisted the plastic lid from Ginny's water bottle and held it to her lips.

'I can't drink that,' she said hazy, recoiling. She tasted the grit of wet graveyard in her mouth.

'I don't have—'

Ginny watched the man, only young, whisking his head around, seeking support.

'I'm okay,' she said pulling her skirt into her lap, sitting up. Seeing her steady made him calm. He took a seat beside her. Ginny looked to the place she had deposited her poem. There was no sign of disturbance. *Why are some things so easy to bury*, she thought, *while other things refuse to die?*

'I come here when things are a bit too much. I find it calming.' His voice was soft.

She noticed a flush rise in his neck. *His blushes must be epic in the sunlight. Poor fulla*, she thought.

'I've noticed her too,' he went on, nodding at the headstone. 'She makes me think about all the life she had that we don't know.'

Ginny looked at him, his straight, fair hair, bowed before the gravestone. He talked differently. Thought differently. A bit like her. 'And if she yearned for more than the sliver she had.'

The man smiled as he fingered the dirt. 'A tomb now suffices him for whom the world was not enough.' He looked up. 'Alexander the Great. Well, not him, exactly. The inscription, on his tomb.' The man raised his knees and hugged them. 'I'm a bit of a nerd.'

'Hence,' Ginny raised her nose into the cemetery.

They chuckled, their breath pushing into the deepening night.

'Reckon that can be true?' she said. 'That the world can fail us? That its expanse, its endless possibilities can be inadequate for the fullness of a single life?'

'Maybe. Why not? If the possibilities are endless ...'

They became silent again. She liked the stillness between them. It felt peaceful.

'Is it even something we can know?' he eventually said. 'I'm not sure I know what day it is most times.'

'There's a pill for that,' Ginny said, gazing at the smoothed patch of dirt between them.

The man stirred. 'Here,' he said reaching into his shirt pocket and pulling out a clump of flowers. White sparks ignited at all angles from an open, round seeded centre. The stems were wrapped in alfoil. Ginny could see a wet tissue poking above the metal base. 'The cockatoos get into the tree out the front. It's Sydney Red Gum. Know the one?'

Ginny nodded.

'Smooth-barked Apple,' he went on. 'They snipped this off this morning, buggers. I come sometimes to sit with Ada,' he nodded to a lopsided headstone towards the side of the wall. 'I like bringing her something, but these belong to you, tonight.'

Ginny took them and twirled the alfoil between her thumb and forefinger. Then she threw her head back and snorted.

'What's so funny?'

'Just life. And death. And the way they can be both and beautiful all at once.' She lifted the bouquet. They stared at the lines of shadow that spread from the blooms in Ginny's hand.

'That's pretty profound. Are you a writer or something?'

'Poet, actually,' she said. 'Newly published, too,' she added.

'Wow. How's that feel?'

'Great for me. Not so good for the trees.'

'So, you're a *murderess* lurking in the graveyard. Of course!'

They laughed.

'Feeling better now?' he asked.

'I feel ... myself,' she replied.

'Well, that's baseline. And better than you appeared when I showed up. Seems my excellent work in restoring the mediocre is done.' He rose.

'Hey, you're not an apparition or something, are you?' Ginny said, still sitting next to the fallen baby gravestone. 'If you are that's okay. I'd just rather know before I watch you dissolve into a grave.'

'Not that I know of,' he said, offering a hand. 'Lachie.'

She grabbed it and pulled herself up. 'Ginny,' she said, rising and brushing the dirt from her skirt.

Lachie turned and began walking to the far wall. 'I have been called a dreamboat, though. Once,' he yelled back to her.

'A dream boat *and* a nerd. Hanging out in a cemetery. What a trifecta,' she called back.

Ginny picked up her backpack and bottle, zipped it closed, then put her arms through the straps. Before leaving, she placed the Red Gum blossoms on the grave face. 'Till next we meet, Dearly Beloved Daughter,' she said. Then, bathed in moonlight, Ginny made her way out of the graveyard and back to the stillness of her home.

Part Three

the ground

36.

I was woken by a blow. Pressure joined Mum's throbbing and my fluid gushed out and away from me. I stopped squiggling around then and became heavy. Like a lump. My head and neck became lodged inside a really tight tunnel so that I couldn't move. I tried kicking my legs around a bit. But they felt so heavy, I got tired and they just flopped. Mum's insides quickly became impossibly small and hotter than I had ever known. All her softness disappeared, and I turned into a stone that was grinding against rippling muscle. I panicked a lot cause Mum's whole body was screaming, trying to push me out. Never in my wildest dreams would I ever have thought that being born was really about getting separated. If I wasn't so scared about all the pushing and beeping and flowing hot surges, I would have been sad about not belonging to Mum's insides anymore.

I knew I had shoulders when they got swallowed by Mum's canal. I was pretty sure I would get jammed, stuck there. Now there was no water in my mouth or nose, and I was trapped cause I was basically a baby chunk, I thought about trying to cry. But then I remembered all Boy Scar's lessons, and how he said Mum would want me to be smart from the moment I was born, so I didn't. Thinking about him really helped me then. It took my mind off my stretching and aching and panicking about being pushed out of Mum and into the outside.

Eventually, my shoulders released and an intense wave of heat and heaviness drove me further down Mum's straining canal. I felt a patch of coldness pool on the crown of my head. I felt my hair for the first time. Its tips waved in the space above me. Mum's insides loosened. It felt strange after all the contorting. Her pushing became pulsing. She did exactly what Boy Scar said she was best known for, she worked with the flow. I had felt it countless times before, with him in Mum's cave, so I knew it was a good sign. In my mind, I could make out her hips, her arms stroking. She sliced her surrounds. Her entire body finding its inside tide, and me riding with her. Rather than it draining from me, she became my water. She let herself flow. And I danced from her womb. Drifting marvellously from inside to out.

At my first gulp of outside air, Mum placed me on her chest. I rested against her clammy skin. She held me gently then started to hum. I felt her lips press against my new wrinkled forehead. Even though I was outside of her, I felt closer than I had ever been.

37.

It took me forever to work out how to ground breathe. Or death think. Or beyond exist. Probably because I was mixed up with charcoal and was flaky and not whole anymore. Most of born baby me lay in a sorrowing, soft heap, thanks to my little girl body being placed on the pyre. It had disintegrated and burned down to ash. Every part except a bit of jaw. And a piece of leg. They were still bones. But only shards. They were the only leftovers that proved I had ever been a me. Something solid that was held and took up space.

I knew my edges had drifted away. Thanks to the burning. Mainly toes and fingers and feet and hands. Plus, my nose. All the cutest parts. They went first cause the fire breeze had lifted them and spread them out a bit. I had to find a way to connect them back to my centre spread if I wanted a new, dead, underground life.

So, I started thinking about each ashy flake and how important they all were and looped a mind rope around them. I made sure to include all the stuff that had sizzled away the furtherest. Like fingernails and eyebrows and things.

I fashioned a memory thread and whizzed it around them all. Mind moving required me to concentrate really hard to zip past and wake all my pieces. I told them, in my zooming, that I was grateful for them being my body and, even though we'd only been a born baby girl for a few months, it was a wonderful and important thing to have been. I thanked them for letting me see clouds and smell oysters and taste milk. For the feeling of being wrapped in fur and hearing the beauty of a melody carried across the waves. My shards had let me taste belonging, smell beauty and hear contentment. They'd held me in the shape of who I was. So, I invited them to be part of what I was to be. My remains started humming when I thought-shared that. Each ash sheet buzzed. The thought rope began shaking and I started vibrating, absorbing the hum and the rattling, resonating with it and my scattered parts.

My melted nose itched. A rush of air memory hurried in and tickled it more. I sniffed in a gigantic surge of air, then sneezed. My cinders exploded. Scattering everywhere. My bits were strewn all over the curve of dirt. I was flung-dusted to every part of the underground bubble. In a single sneeze in my grave, I became part of the everything.

The earth pocket's walls were low. My tomb was mostly smooth and cosy. A mixture of dirt and a bit of sand and some smoothish rock. I liked how different these places felt. The dirt was strong. There was lots of it. All brown and full and spreading. It looked rich, but since I hadn't lived long enough I couldn't be sure it was good soil.

Bumps of mustard-gold sandstone pushed through the brownness. In some parts, the rock was soft enough to crumble and yellow sand danced with the dark earth and made a lighter powdery soil. Those bits of grave were bright. And snug. The more I sprinkled on them, the more I loved it.

Because I didn't have skin or blood or organs anymore, the dampness didn't worry me. I was glad it was there. It was what made all the life grow. Families of mould mottled the walls of the grave. Each splatter had a bunched centre that freckled into a pretty pattern. Their outer specks glowed silvery green in the darkness. They were fuzzy and splotchy and elegant. I thought that those mould splats were places where the dead and the living danced. That's probably why I loved them so much. Whenever I stared at them for a while, I swore they would start twinkling at me. I suppose I saw stars when I was a baby. I can't remember them if

I did. But the mould of my grave became the first stars I knew really.

There was also lichen growing. It burst in dainty florets on the sandstone. The tufts were grey-green with yellow squirts. To look at them, you would think they were scratchy and hard, but really their flakes were spongey. I was pretty sure lichen was probably the breath of dark, wet underground things. Or maybe it was a sweat patch. I laughed at the thought of rocks sweating, cause they were oafish and heavy and couldn't move themselves around much, so that lichen hair was growing in their funk. It's weird to think now that most people believe a grave is still and unmoving. In reality, it's full of dead things squirming and shifting all over the place. Lots of things grow in graves. And disintegrate. And are born all over again.

Having no body made a lot more things possible. In my mind scatter I held out a tastebud and put it to a lichen patch. It felt fluffy. But tasted flat. My tongue memory told me its flakes were spongey. And I was part of that sponginess somehow. It felt nice tickling the folds of softness and letting that softness also be the edges of me. I allowed the idea of me to melt into the flakes. I was pleased my remains could be useful. It made being dead worth it. Plus, I didn't need myself anymore.

Hugged by dirt and carried by rock, I decided existing in the blooming might be wonderful. I stared and stared and stared at the mould splats and lichen stains, and I forgot where they started and I began. Soon it became all I had ever been and wanted to become.

I had been stare-dreaming at the mould star-splats for lifetimes when a noise rumbled into my ground. My dirt ash shook a bit when it did, then tumbled about in a flimsy, flopping way. I sifted through myself for a listening bit and pressed it to the floor. Maybe it was just the dirt stretching. I thought I heard a faraway grumbling. A low dronish corridor of sound. But I couldn't be sure. It was a bit strange trying to use ears I didn't have any more. I tried to strain deeper beneath the ground, but the sound had gone. I settled back into my scattered self amongst the dirt and dust, and gazed at the roof. Cheeky mould spots poked out their dotted tongues. I imagined folding my burnt hands behind my scorched skull and smiling and scrunching my melted nose at the naughty shapes above me.

I can't say how long after that the insects came. First only a few trickled in. Then heaps arrived. Armies. In formation. They surged and streamed in. Ants, slaters, cockroaches and centipedes emerged from the ceiling and walls. Each sprinkled granules of dirt onto the floor. And into sifted, diffused me. They trampled all over the mould. Some even bit off chunks of lichen as they scuffed themselves through its fanning edges. I thought about squishing a few that traipsed over my remains with a burnt-up fist, but of course I couldn't. Their crappy dirt trails and cascading falls only muddled me up and weakened me even more. The mould and lichen immediately reached out and patched up the newly made bug entry points. That annoyed me, cause it would only be keeping them in and that meant I had to put up with their scurrying and scampering about. A string of ants walked over my leg shard to get to a crevice in the cove joint.

'Oi,' I yelled. 'That's my leg you're trampling over.'

They didn't respond. They just kept their heads down and kept marching in. And around. Everywhere.

'Bum sniffers,' was all I could think to say as they clambered over a part of me. 'Poo eaters,' I added because I was getting fed up. And cramped. And diluted. And technically, they sort of were.

Every new creature that scrambled over me and my grave then found a place of their own. Eventually, they stopped scuttling around and settled. Some amongst the folds of moss, some in the crooks of a wall join, others between grains of soil or dirty sand. One slater coiled itself into a ball amongst my ashes and used me as some sort of blanket.

'That's out of the question,' I said, trying to pull my powdery borders away. But of course, I didn't move. She just snuggled further into me. All I could do was sigh and notice the algae, that now throbbed a sleeping green, was highlighted with twinkling flecks of metallic brown. Exoskeletons flickered from between the soil as my grave became still again. But smaller. And crowded.

After the infestation, I forgot what silence was. The insects started chewing and spitting and licking and didn't stop. Ever. The sound of them munching and salivating was pretty disgusting. Gross. And incessant. It was wet and private and made me uncomfortable. Plus, I was worried they would eat all the beautiful green patterning I was now part of. I saw a lot of them nibble at the mould. When I caught an ant pooing in the lichen, I forced all my effort into a yell. But no noise came out. If anything, some of me just spilled further into the dirt. Even though my ears had been singed off, I could still hear close-sounding things. Their mouths smacked and licked and nibbled and sucked non-stop. I really wished I couldn't hear anything then.

If I had to pick a favourite from all the new interlopers, I would have said I liked the ants the best. They were the quietest by far. And every time they passed each other, they would meet and touched heads, running their antennae over the other's face. This touch looked gentle. But quick. A caress, but rushed. That's what I liked about them. They were nice to each other. Unlike the others, they didn't pretend they were the only insect that existed in the world.

After a long time, I witnessed an ant funeral. A string of ants emerged from a hole in the ground. One came to the surface with a body on its back. The neighbouring ant met the carrier and caressed its head and feelers. Together they lifted the body from one back and onto the other. The new carrier then took the body on to the next ant. And so, it went down the line until they arrived at a nook between sandstone and the dirt.

All the ants gathered, and the body was laid down. They moved forward and cleaned it, removing all the dirt and moss and mould they could. After all the caressing, they formed a line and left. Ants kept visiting the body, fussing and propping it up for a long time afterwards. In fact, when the next ant died, everything was repeated and the second body laid carefully next to the first. Watching how they remembered and cared about the ones that had died made me want to cry. But my eyeballs had melted a long time ago, so I had no tear-making stuff to do it with. Instead, I thought about sadness and how sharing it is sort of beautiful. I was grateful sorrow existed, which is weird because by itself it can be terrible. Painful. But the ants reminded me that sharing sadness made a difference. Their burials were beautiful because they gathered to help. And to care. I hoped my funeral was something like that when I'd died and was buried.

I was watching a centipede, wondering if each of its legs had its own brain, when I heard the taps. The sound was strong. And much clearer than the rumbling I had heard before. At first, they were single taps. Spaced out and clear, as if drawing attention.

I told the insects to stop squirming and be still as the taps became louder. They kept doing what they wanted cause I couldn't talk.

I mind-shifted myself into the dirt a bit further. I squiggled, hoping to feel the beat. Maybe become it. A full, high clap broke into the grave like a wave. Its strength dislodged part of the roof. A lump of claggy mud fell and hit my powder part, splattering me even more. I watched a cunning cockroach gather a couple of my cinders and whisk them off to its nest. Then the taps changed into cluster clacks. A flurry of beats came quickly. Then disappeared just as fast. Their rhythm felt like a question floating in the dirt. If I still had had a heartbeat, I know it would have fluttered. With fright. Or excitement. Or maybe just in response. I looked to the insects hoping for some kind of support. They weren't interested though, choosing to continue their ferreting without a care for what I thought or did.

The tapping gradually got louder, as if the sound was about to breech through the soil. Then, after one huge clack, the time slipped into a regular double beat. It locked in and didn't budge.

The stronger second beat brought cascades of dirt down on top of me. The ceiling shook, and a dust cloud began to linger in the grave as the dirt and soil pulsed in the pocket. The ground underneath me was slipping away. Soon, the loose dirt revealed a sharp, straight corner of dense orange block. Further beating dusted excess soil from a shorter lip and second heavy corner. Dirt cascaded and uncovered a protruding platform. It was then that the tapping stopped.

The sound revealed a shape. A long box. It was hard. And solid. Straight. Unlike anything I had ever seen. I looked at the thing and, in my mind scatter, asked, 'What are you?'

The block seemed to have no living bits; no mind juice to slosh ideas around in or talking bits to get stuff out. No tongue or teeth to make words with. But it told me it was a brick. I thought it a weird type of word, all sharp and harshish, like the very way it looked. Through my eye ash, I looked at it. Granules of sand covered its tough orange skin. I noticed a chip of bleached shell compacted into its side. It was a cockle. I knew about them when I was a baby, cause Mum's milk was cockle-flavoured sometimes. Also, when I was tired and wrapped in her arms next to a fire, an empty cockle would flit into my almost dream and bobble in the water, its ridges catching the sun's rays and reflecting them into the greenness as it rested amongst the currents. It would drift and I would follow into gentle, baby rest. That's how I knew it was cockle. Cause it knew me. I tried the word again. 'Brick.' It felt angular. Closed. I didn't like it. I tried it again. 'Brick.' Sharp. Heavy. Hard. 'Brick.' Harsh. 'Brick.' An end. A barrier. A wall.

'But,' I said to no one, as the slaters and roaches climbed, 'you're just clay, aren't you? Yes, I'm sure you are. You look it.'

I took in the amber and red-yellow body. 'Bemul.'

The rigidity of the box released. As if it were listening.

I went on. 'You're earth. Like I am.'

I sensed the brick further soften.

'I was covered in you. Almost every day. A man's clay-covered face was the last thing I saw. With eyes. When I had them.'

Keeping its heft, the brick opened its pores. De-solidified. Its particles cleared space within its solidness. That's how I knew it remembered me too.

'I know you more than you know yourself,' I told it. My words were thick and flying. Because it was nothing more than water and land and I had been both since forever. I added, 'That makes me your Elder, Brick. You rise from my ashes. You exist because of me.'

Remembering itself and claiming me as kin, the solid, protruding block relented. It opened. And I entered it. Through our kinship, immediately, I multiplied. Surging into every block and brick, clay vein and ochre deposit that ever had been. I travelled to them without moving. I multiplied within them without repeating. I lived inside each without breathing. I rose in every ruin and rubble and towering pile that had ever been conceived or modelled or shaped in this place. I became their centre. Their building block. Their architectural essence. Bricks were my first propagation. Through them, I transformed into outside and in. I grew ears again. I heard and held all that was ever said and done and planned and schemed and hidden and promised and learned. In a matter of moments, I became safety, shelter. Fortune. Belonging. I was made to house everything inside of me.

38.

Cawing Aunty Yellowtails

When Ginny spotted the toy car on the footpath, she scooped it up and dropped it into her bag. At home, she placed it on her kitchen table and stared. Palm-sized, only a skerrick of powder-blue paint remained on its body. Most of it had chipped away, revealing the plain wood underneath. The block that served as the bumper bar was scuffed in its corners, but all its wooden wheels still worked, and were still sturdy.

Ginny shook it. The pins holding the wheels tinkled a bit, but she could tell it was old and was made to last. She ran it over the tabletop. The movement was smooth. She circled a few figure eights, then put her chin on the table, bringing the toy to her eye line. It could have been as old as her. Older. But it knew what it was. It was a toy car with or without a child to play with, or a hand zooming it around, with or without all the spit and sound effects, inside and outside a toy box or day care. It was itself and nothing more.

Ginny sighed.

She yearned for the same simplicity, a clarity of purpose in her own life. 'I wish I was a block,' she said into the open kitchen. 'I could block with the best of em,' she went on. 'I'm pretty solid,' she added slapping her bum, then chuckling at its wobble. 'I could handle a kid—'

Her insides went numb. Looking at the toy motionless on the table, she invited dull nothingness to overtake her. It was her punishment. And she deserved to feel it.

The new moon shone a bright whiteness as she walked to the day care at the end of her street. Reaching over the childproof gate, she popped its latch and walked in. The centre proper with its heavy wooden door was locked, but access to the front courtyard was readily available, if you were adult-sized. Momentum took her to the *Stroller Parking* sign to the left of the centre's entrance. Three dishevelled prams were stacked beneath it. Walking, she noticed the dried Weet-Bix and pulverised biscuit cakings of their capsules. Guided by moonlight, Ginny moved past the last pram and to the end of the orange pavers. Beyond was the building's corner and a side alley, its scrap of dirt beginning beneath another childproof gate. Ginny crouched in the cramped corner and steadied herself on the gate for support. She scratched at the ground, making a small depression. She reached into her bra and pulled out the page.

But she stopped. Again, she had walked out without her full, ready, water bottle. It was probably still on the kitchen bench. Swearing as she scanned the courtyard, Ginny clocked a drink bottle in the pram's undercarriage. She took it and shook.

'Yes!' she said, popping its lid and shaking droplets onto her page. When it was wet enough, she chucked the bottle back and placed the paper in the hole.

Cawing Aunty Yellowtails

Head bowed, buried in work, Yellowtails caw
Descending a curved beaked chorus upon my crown
Tri-patterned cries still my fingers and well
Brackish overflow upon cheeks plain
So elevated, buried, resonant their tune

Gold-flecked shadows cry with me within forever blue
I want them to descend
Replace claw with femur, wing with ulna
And, wobbling fat with spiralling ancestry,
Walk into my kitchen and make me a cup of tea

the belburd

Would that skin-sagged, bone-bulged finger-wings place
In my wordless hands cups
Of warm kinship. In seeding skirts and drooping bras
Would that they rub my back between sips and hug me
And my sorrow-laden, post-parental state

Cawing Aunty Yellowtails that make cups of tea
As well as bring the rain, taste pain on high breezes,
Soothe aches of writing in a stranger's tongue,
Ease stings of severance from mother's nature
My airborne aunts serenade compassion into me

ginny dilboong

Covering the words, she pushed the stroller's wheels over the mound to compact it tightly. Ginny then walked to the front door of the centre. The bluestone step held a pool of moonwash over its matt surface. She bent and placed the wooden block in its centre and, thinking hard about the wooden truck, the full moon, the stroller parking bay and all those simple, silent, life-flooded things, walked towards home.

39.

There was movement at the far end of the ground. And the wet rustling sound of millions of legs. A shimmer arose from the lower curve of earth and a mass of flowing wriggliness spilled from the corner.

I moved into the insect stream to see closer but was twirled and spun and trodden on from within. I dispersed into bits of a lichen tuft spackled on the roof. From there, I watched gleaming slater backs twinkle and surge like the surface of some great water body. The mould enjoyed the spectacle also, giggling and waving to the crawling, coursing tide. Slater ripples rolled in the flowing current. Patches of stillness reflected and shone. The river was magnificent. Streaming and gushing and rolling by.

That's when I saw her. A haze baby – kicking her chubby, fresh legs from a possum fur blanket. She lay beside the water, cooing and smiling at the mould patterns above.

She was round, with short brown curls. Her arms glistened. A necklace of baby river reeds rested against her chest. I leaned into the image of her. As I did, she blossomed, rolling from her back and readying as if to crawl. I lurched forward, wondering if I should stop her as she rocked on her knees then inched towards the stream. She stopped short of the flowing bank and, lying full on her belly, ran her hands through the flow. A grey rise crested and trickled over her arm.

She grew again, this time a girl, sitting at the edge of the scurrying stream. She began playing, sketching an image in the dust. Her thin wrists curved wondrous arches as her fingers tickled me, and the dirt. When she finished, she sat on her heels, this time growing again. The young girl, her hair now long and thick with curls, leaned into the surge and cupped her hands. Slate water dripped from them as she rubbed her face and then the back of her neck. I watched insects drip from her fingers and right themselves before running on. Then she gathered her hair on her shoulder, growing once more as she did. Running her hands through it, she pulled forward shells that were fixed in its strands. She inspected them. As she rewound the shells back into place, she surged again. Now a young woman, she flicked loose shells and stray strands into the water. The droplets caused ripples on the water's surface.

Teems of slaters surrounded then swallowed the offcasts in the flow.

Rising, she rubbed her scalp and shook the ends of her hair lightly. She stood, then held out an open hand. A girl ran up and clasped it. Together, they walked hand in hand upstream. Slowly the haze lifted, and they and the river disappeared. I moved onto a sprinkle of self near brick. A centipede perched on top of a brick was extending itself from the platform in an elongated stretch. Its antennae wriggled in the air, encouraging me to retrace the movements of the growing baby-woman and girl. I followed the line they made. The path she had walked now had mangrove stalks emerging from the bare earth. Very few of these smallish, pointing fingers grew into leafy, juvenile shrubs. Upside-down tufts of foliage with pink belled blooms hung from the ceiling directly above where she had sat and played. *How glorious*, I thought, *to witness and be a part of something that can never die.*

Then, perhaps as confirmation, a breeze stirred and rustled through the upside-down wildflowers clinging to the roof. They waved and wafted, their movement sprinkling a dusting of dirt into the grave. A sheening, fat cockroach pushed out from the wall and poked its head into the air. It waved its front legs around in it. Its claw tips fluttered. Then it folded its legs and licked along their entire length. By the time the creature had finished grooming itself, the walls and roof were filling with germinating plants. Pinks and oranges and purples and bluebells sprouted through a network of bacterial must. Three slaters wobbled their way to a lichen cluster on a protruding sandstone rise. After walking in a circle a few times, they hunched their backs and pushed out a stream of tiny pellets into the lichen's centre. After this, they toddled to opposing parts of the grave.

Shit, I thought, *is perfect fertiliser.* I looked around my newly growing landscape. *Decay seems to be the building block of life.*

There were hubs of activity inside the grave. Thanks to the lichen, the rocks were spongey, so I took to bouncing on them and jumping from one to the other. Something about the feeling of being encased in ruffling folds felt wonderful to me. It didn't matter they were oftentimes damp and cold. It was a fun way to practice moving. The freedom of bouncing on those underground moss beards as trampolines was magnificent.

The more I jumped, the more I wanted to know what was beneath. I started trying to squelch beneath the lichen's folds. Rather than stop at the crumples of moss, I searched for the pores of rock they grew upon. I tried to enter them. Eventually I worked it out. I had to approach from the top and the side. A bit lichen and a bit dirt. That was the magic formula for getting sandstone to open.

When rock swallowed parts of me and I was absorbed, everything hard turned to sponge. But inside the sandstone I felt gathered and strong. Solid again. I was grateful the stone lent itself to me in this way. Below the rock surface, I lined up all the breach points. Each tuft of lichen pulsated intense, underground green. And in each centre tuft, a ruby heart glowed.

The puddles of green and red shone a pathway beyond the pocket of grave. This continued into the everywhere. The red centres beckoned. Perhaps I could reverse jump into them as well. But how to get to each of them from inside rock? I thought hard. There was only dirt between the way points. Nothing solid I could melt into or become. I started to feel trapped. Enclosed. Buried beneath a burial. I knew I was panicking but had no way to feel it. No breath or heartbeat to fight against. No body to tell me to run. Or cry. Or punch. Inside rock, I could do nothing.

Just then, I felt the sandstone smile. Or stretch. Or hug me maybe. The idea of nothing filled me and brought its own shining centre. Letting the need for form disappear, I disintegrated myself. In that state of nothingness, I found

I could swirl amongst soil and through stone, surge within boulder and squelch inside clay. Using the red pathway, I moved to the end of the grave. When I did, I noticed insect droppings illuminated gold and violet and midnight blue. I decided then, being a soaring every-nothing was the most glorious thing that ever could be.

I rose through the ground from the bedrock and soil to surface next to brick.

'That was easier than I thought,' I said to myself, laying on its sandy face. I felt centred and slow, despite having nothing to me. I collapsed into my nothing gut to stare at the once was insect river. The dirt had been washed away to reveal rows of bricks lining the grave ground.

Throngs of creatures emerged from between the rows to ferret and wiggle their bums about. I soaked into a couple of sandstone rises to get closer. Rows of new brick curved into the grave floor. Each line was its own specific colour. Trails of yellow, both bright and fading, stretched towards the wall and dipped beneath it, eventually being swallowed by the dirt again. Burnt orange formations followed the same path. A delicate row of slightly smaller apricot blocks made the top of the new ground floor curve. They seemed friendly enough. And kind too. But because I had only just learned how to be nothing and liked how it felt, and I didn't really want another adventure just yet, I rested upon the new brick channel and watched cycles of upside-down flowers sprout then blossom and bloom then die.

I turned to the arrangement of bricks, eventually. I stared. Their gentle orange was exquisite. An even spreading of clay and sand made their textures strong and smooth. Looking down their pathway I wondered at their positioning. It didn't allude or point or encourage to anywhere that I could see.

They must be covering something, I thought. I decided to seep through them and see if I was right. I went beneath their surface and emerged into a tunnel. Its length was cavernous. And dark. At its base a stream trickled. Water flowed along an uneven floor. It acted much as the slater stream did. Rippling. Rustling. Running. As I listened to the drips and gargles, I saw that the base of the tunnel was made by slabs of sandstone. Bricks but in much bigger, older form. Each block was pockmarked or chipped, and the water seemed to roll gleefully over the blemishes as it continued on its way.

Splashes of water dripped in the distance. The tunnel's bricks and blocks snaked for ages. And the thin stream wound all the way along. Block gave way to line, which then became a single point in the distance, eventually overtaken by darkness. A shiver quivered through my nothingness. I had never seen so much distance before. Or a pathway that had been ready-made and open, the way this one was now. I knew I didn't want to return through the bricks and back to my grave. Something told me that the grave was a place of the past for me now. And that unknown things and newness was what my future should be.

A thickish Red Gum root protruded from the tunnel's side. I knew that meant a tree would grow, and spread to overtake the grave.

'If I fail to harness my new nothingness and leave parts of me where I can in the everything,' I told myself, 'I will only exist and then expire. Without a soul to know or to care for me.'

I wondered if I could send my spirit into it and join in its flow.

Above me, a rustle tickled the young leaves on the growing mangrove shrubs. The shocks of inverted grass shimmied. The plants on the roof of my grave tingled and grew. Veins of fat, green succulents pierced through the wall and rooted in runs. Bright magenta faces heavy with needle-thin petals flecked amongst the new growth. In my disseminated state, I saw the sprouting taking place in my grave and cried at its beauty. Without eye or tear.

A banksia pushed its way into and then out of my earthen pocket, its middle bursting with orange flower heads and serrated leaves. And directly above me, a Red Gum grew. Its sprawling roots pushing upwards a thick trunk weeping red sap. Bark peeled as the tree grew and collected at its base. Creatures picked amongst the debris.

'I should now like to transform,' I announced to my grave, with great tenderness.

I watched as a butterfly emerged from a clinging clump of upside-down grass. Its flight to a neighbouring cluster triggered the release of a kaleidoscope more.

'It's time for my spirit to grow wings,' I said. 'It's right that now I fly.'

A rumble filled the tunnel's chamber. I shuddered as grit fell from between the bricks. A second growl stirred. Its vibration sent insects scurrying. They scattered, inside and out of the tunnel, in all directions. Their network, I realised then, extended much further than I had ever thought before. The shuddering gathered power, shaking the entire underground. Then a clunking cascade pushed towards me from the far end of the tunnel. A wave of water surged, and the end of the tunnel collapsed. The weight of the falling bricks triggered a chain reaction. Within moments, the tunnel was in pieces as sludge gathered below. Then a monstrous pylon pierced the rubble and jutted upwards, its impossibly sharp tip skewering all in its path.

The pylon was sleek and shining grey, its metallic sheen unlike anything else amongst the underground. Its shaft was broad and flat, its perimeter shining and sharp. I don't know why, but I licked it. Every particle of my nothingness quivered.

The taste was a dull thudding. Its flavour was delicious. I went this time to kiss the steel, but as I shifted, the ground gave way. The cascading earth pulled me into its slipstream, and I tumbled, sucked down to hurtle through the dirt. My descent finished with me strewn across the teeth of an underground drill. Ground sandstone slurry caked the spaces between sets of rock shattering teeth. These teeth, the shape of cones, were fashioned at different angles and positioned on the end of a machine. The cones were kelp shells, pointed at the tip and curling into a wide base. These were stuck all over the end of the machine. I soaked myself between the ground-up stone and into the machine's teeth. Within moments, the motor whirred, and the drill began rotating. I buzzed and jerked as I cut into the bedrock, the teeth of the machine pulverising the stone and reducing it to dust. At first, it was uncomfortable making foundations crumble and dissolve. But the carving and resistance of the stone had me feeling stronger, more substantial than I had ever felt. Surging through rock made me more powerful with every shuddering advance.

I was harpooned by a metal rod and shot into the air. I was then pierced by a stake. As I was bored into, a high-pressured jet of water doused my passage and allowed the securing of a bolt at the end of the rod. Parts of me were secured by the rock bolt. Tightened, sealed, never to leave.

While bits of me continued to grind through the sandstone, other parts mixed with the rock spoil falling from the drill head. I took this moment to sprinkle as much of my spirit self as I could amongst the newly made powder. I grew again and spread. I flung parts of myself into as much matter as I could. I decided I should also melt into the rock pores again, absorb myself in its breath and push further and deeper away. As I moved through it, the elements of the rock changed. Eventually I slowed. It was dense and hard to move. There was no grave or cave or pocket or place to rest and think in. I was now foundation, and foundation was everywhere.

An age later, parts of my nothingness were excavated and pulverised. This me was whizzed down a conveyor belt and flung on a pile to be heated and shaped. My form was moulded, bent, cooled, and beaten. Finally, I was hauled into the above.

Sunlight blinded me. The air tasted of smog. I smelled salt mixed with water and concrete. I knew I had wings. They were made of steel and were flying and reaching into the air over many places. I stretched across bends and folds of sand and beach I felt I had known. I extended my steel branches in greeting to the everything around.

40.

The Dusky Bell

Stepping into the cafe, she could feel something was different. Immediately her eyes were drawn to the display fridges – three hulking, chilled, cream-filled windows with shelves packed with pastry, icing, sponge and meringue. Surveying all the sweetness, Ginny waited, expecting tears to well. None came. She walked towards the glazed fruit beaming at her from its custard and pastry casing. Nothing. She bent towards the slices of black forest gateau. Her heart rate, she felt, stayed steady. She felt only calm.

She thought she would chance it and order a coffee. She moved to the counter and ordered her usual.

'Have here,' she added before tapping her card.

The barista looked at her. 'I'll have it brought over.'

Ginny chose the table closest to the cake displays. There she could not only see but smell the sweetness. She looked at the icing-dusted tray of vanilla slices and sat down. Their layered, flaking pastry had no effect. She looked at the cannoli on the bottom shelf. Same reaction – nothing. A girl came over and placed a small glass and a carafe of water on the table in front of her.

'Oh thanks,' Ginny said.

'No worries,' replied the girl. 'Having in? You're usually a takeaway.'

'Yeah,' said Ginny looking at her. She was young, probably still school age. Ginny noticed the ends of a tattoo sneaking out from her sleeve.

'Almond latte, no sugar, usually in a pink keep cup. That's you, isn't it?'

Ginny smiled.

'I've got a good memory. Ginny, isn't it?'

'Wow!'

'I remember cause Little Lucas Latte-Art over there always mucks it up. Don't worry,' she added, bowing closer. 'It's not just you, he screws everyone's name up. You told him Jenny to make it easier for him and he actually started calling you Jade. Now you just say belburd. He gets that cause he's a dodo.'

They both laughed. 'You do have a good memory, maybe you should change your line of work, get into poker or something a bit more lucrative.'

'Yeah, I've thought that too sometimes. But I like it here. I like people. Coffee and bringing out the best in people.'

Near the espresso machine, Ginny's order was called out. The girl spun away and returned, placing the full cup and saucer in front of her.

'So why have here today? What's changed?'

Ginny looked at the smooth, warm liquid, the white froth luscious and thick on top. She picked it up. 'I don't know.' She sipped.

'Well, you look heaps different. Sort of like ...' She turned. 'That.' She pointed.

'What? Floppy layers of streaky brown?'

'No,' the girl said quickly. 'Regal, like Opera Cake.'

'Gee, thanks,' Ginny replied.

'Could have been a tart.'

They laughed together again.

'Whatever has changed, I think it's a good thing. See ya, belburd,' the girl said, spinning on her heels and returning to the register.

Ginny sipped her coffee. She knew what the girl was on about. She felt it too. For months she had avoided the shop altogether. The memories of her and Nath slouched into each other, watching passers by, were too much for her. The colours were too much. The sweetness only served to remind her of everything she had lost. Today was the first day in a long time she could look at the place and not cry. Today the cakes just looked like cakes and not lost helpings of promise and sweetness and desire. She rifled through her duffel bag.

'Yes,' she said, loudly, so that a bike-riding, short-black-sipping MAMIL in a backwards riding cap shuddered in fright.

Ginny pulled out a piece of handmade paper and rustled around for a pen. Slapping her notebook on the table, she transcribed the poem.

The Dusky Bell

crumbled mustard paves the unchanging trail
bracken curled fronds hint a pathway
angophora and turpentine giants breathe dappled sun
onto boulders of lichen
undergrowth arranged in skink scratched highways
the dusky bell grows and bows

delicate sisters humble their heads casting
downward blushes into tongue-lashed branch
huddling leaves of licked kinship proclaim
'she's back' and I stop
the dusky bell sees through subterranean root
the change budding within me

flushed chamber encases a golden-teared trickle

grief suspended, thick and peering in beautiful bush

the dusky bell had known me and declared

my return before even I knew myself

gratefully lost in her ancient paths

meeting my own reconstruction in the bend of her bloom

ginny dilboong

When she finished, Ginny dabbed water from the carafe on the paper and folded it into a square. She downed her coffee and stood, winking at the cakes as she walked past them and towards the bathroom in the shop's rear yard. Crouching, she dug a hole and planted the poem.

Ginny ran her hands under the cubicle tap then walked to the cafe's entrance. The young girl smiled as she made her way out.

'You know my name, what's yours?' Ginny asked.

'Fuschia.'

'Thanks for noticing, Fuschia. See you round.' Feeling light as cream and sweet as honey, Ginny stepped out of the cafe and into the street.

41.

The me that was fashioned into an arch is so deep a grey that I appear black. My darkness sparkles with winks of silver, as if a billion stars are trapped inside my colour. And, of course, they are. Stars and paint and melted rock and rust, I am all of it. Stardust and steel. You'll forgive me if I tell you that my beauty is quite well regarded. It is widely spoken of. As is my strength. I give meaning and pull focus. I accentuate and define. I am my mother in that regard. Being made into a bridge and painstakingly pieced together over the great waterway means I can see it all. I look through my foundations and cradle time in my hands. Just as I easily peer into future sunrises. My view from here is endless. And I am grateful.

In this form I look upon her first, each day. She continues as she always does. Hugging the edges of her waterways. Fishing or cooking or repairing her nets. Occasionally, she throws oyster shells at passengers on the ferries. Or makes fun of women tottering in high heels as they run for the bus. Delighting in commotion, she will sometimes cause a crash or delay or pile up. She loves making this as early as she is able, and when she does, she laughs all day long.

I thought for a time she wouldn't recognise me in this form, but one day she caught mackerel and cooked it on her fire, then brought it to the bottom of my pylon and rubbed its fat into my granite base. That's when I knew she had seen me. And still loved me, although I was only months old when we both died. The oil of the fish made its way into my wing feathers, and I preen them. It also feeds the rivets that hold my bones in place. When Mum settles on her favourite beach for the night, I send a soft wind to keep her fire stoked. Or a cool one on the nights that still hold the heat.

'Good morning, Daughter, and thank you,' are her first words to me each day.

I love my mother more than words or songs or nets will ever show.

Sometimes my sister will join her. They pry oysters and dig cockles together. I recognised her the first moment a shell glinted from her hair. Sister's hair is always wonderful. Glossy and long and full of bounce. She washes it with clay and rinses it to make it shine. Sometimes she massages animal fat into her scalp. She tends Mother's hair also, binding it in just a way or securing teeth into it with gum. My sister is as beautiful as our mother, and I am so proud of her. I love leaving little gifts in her way. An echidna quill or section of reed for her nose. And always the most colourful, shimmering shells for her hair. Great Whale brings me the best ones. He always keeps an eye out for me as he travels the waters of the coastline. Often, I'll carry them on the north running tides from the pretty, white sand beaches in the south. I put part of me in them too so she can fix me to her. The world is glorious from my sister's shoulders. In exchange, Great Whale has me reporting on the movement of ships and whales that convoy along the coast.

'Of course, I can hear them as they sing their travelling songs, but I can't see them, Sprite, as well as you can,' he always says. 'What are the numbers like this season, or this day?'

All I loved are in my breath, and I am in theirs. When they eat at their fires, I am with them in the flames and the smouldering coals that embrace them. I am in the water they drink and the words they speak, and the dreams they make at night. And not just theirs. I am in everything, old and new. I am the sound of the belburd as it rings through the world. I am the cars and trucks and trains. I am the birds with jet engines. I am trams and sand that has been heated into the glass of your windows and computer screens and mobile phones. I am the concrete and metal of all the new pathways, bridges and overpasses, tunnels and causeways, and I'm the rock that is removed and sold to make them. I am in trees and paper and the shape of ideas. I am words and ink and have been waiting so that you should know. No longer am I a sprite. Or a spit or splat. Or a scatter of ash. I am heiress. Your mistress. The builder and built. Everything you have and see in this place is because of me. I am the universe, the belburd. Everything, even you, is because of me.

42.

the belburd

Ginny Dilboong swept a towel from the rack in the bathroom and jammed it into her beach bag. Then she jumped in her car. She was going to her favourite strip of beach to sunbathe and finish her poem. Nathan was a dickhead and had left her exactly when she needed him. She would finish her poem and get her tan on, then let him go. Forever.

'Dark and deadly,' she scoffed, remembering their first meeting. Plugging her charger cord into the console, she scrolled down her O.G. playlist. Passing Erykah and Whitney then Ella and Aretha, she added, 'I've got a million other things to do with my time.' Her thumb hovered over Chaka Khan. 'And ovaries for that matter.' She turned the ignition and pressed play. As the flourish of strings and seventies disco beat of the first bars of 'I'm Every Woman' began, Ginny looked at herself through the rear-view mirror. She had paid a huge price being with him. She almost didn't recognise herself.

'I definitely need a soak,' she told herself, picturing the exact spot of beach she was planning to lay her towel. 'Wash it away. Start again.' As the song built, the chorus kicked in. Ginny zoomed off, belting the lyrics into the car.

When she hit the Anzac Bridge, she wound down the window and sang at the top of her lungs. She kept singing as she merged lanes and crossed the harbour.

At the carpark, Ginny swung her bag over her arm and picked along the pathway to the sand. She found her patch and spread out her towel. She jiggled out of her shorts and shirt and shoved them under her towel. Adjusting her bikini, she took out her red notebook and thumbed through its pages. Taking up the pen, she asked through the deepest of breaths for the beach and the shade and the waves and the water to help her find the words and rhythm to write.

When sweat hit her brow and her skin began to tingle, Ginny tore out the page and walked into the water.

On her banks, a crow opens its wings and flaps a charcoal shine into a blue above. A gridlocked driver checks emails then runs into the car in front. A boy stacks it from his scooter, grazing both palm and pride. A caged bird whistles at its reflection in a mirror. A horse snorts. A cat stalks a baby lorikeet on its first flight from its nest. A rat dashes along failing fence palings to pluck a fig from a tree. A train carriage beeps and closes graffiti-caked doors. A cheating couple writhes upon cold hotel bedsheets. A painter raises brush to canvas, then withdraws and leaves the room. A long-haul flight lands. An ibis pecks at a half-closed rubbish bin, and a woman borrows books from a library. An old man laughs. A teen rises on tips of toes to steal a bottle of perfume. And somewhere in the always, a newly born baby takes her final, shallow breath.

After wetting her hair, Ginny released her embryonic
lines into the surface of the water. She watched the
ink run and the paper crumple and fold. Eventually it
sank and scraped against the grains. It tickled my arm.
I smiled then sent a kiss of breeze to her forehead. She
wiggled her fingers as it caressed her face.
I was proud of fledging in the sand of her shallows.
Because she was wonderful. And fierce.
And funny and brave. She had been broken.
But had remade and I was grateful I was part
of her. And we were the belburd.
Soaring though cycles of loss
and rebirth.
Inside, above,
under.
Continuing.
Always.

Author's Note

In 1791, Cammeraygal fisherwoman and cultural leader Barangaroo gave birth to a baby girl on the southern shores of Sydney Harbour. The baby was her third child but her first to Wangal ceremonial leader Woollarawarre Bennelong, after losing her first family to the Port Jackson smallpox epidemic of 1789.

Barangaroo died shortly after giving birth and the baby, named Dilboong (the Sydney Aboriginal word for *Manorina melanophrys*, bell minor or bellbird), only lived a matter of months. Bennelong performed burial rites over his daughter, cremating her, then burying her ashes in the same grave where he had deposited his wife's remains only weeks earlier. Their graves, originally in the grounds of the governor's residence, are now covered by the bitumen of Bridge Street and the Museum of Sydney.

Two years ago, I overheard a conversation on a Sydney train. Three women were speaking about house hunting in the Sydney market. As I eavesdropped, I became frustrated.

What they attributed to fate, luck and the abundance of the universe I saw as blindness to affluence and privilege. As the train pulled away from Redfern station, I searched for my own understanding. Immediately, my mind went to that little baby. The daughter of the first sovereign couple of the colony. To me, she held all the riches of new and old Sydney. With Dilboong calling, I began to dream the beginning of the book you hold now.

For research, I visited all the places connected to what I knew of Dilboong's story. I walked the shores of her mother's Country, ferreting along the edges of Collins Flat Beach, Sirius Cove and Manly foreshore. I also walked the harbour's opposing shoreline, drifting amongst the places her father lived – Bennelong Point, Circular Quay, Me-Mel (Goat Island) and the southern edges of the Parramatta River. I spent time in the grounds of a small Catholic church in the Rocks where bronze busts of Bennelong and Barangaroo frame the entrance. And I sat in front of a house in a quiet cul-de-sac in Putney, paying respects to Bennelong in his grave, sealed beneath a suburban road.

This story had me communing with time and change, and the nature of their effect. I have always thought time separates and severs – it carves moments from a whole. When you measure in terms of generations and continuing cycles, carving is destructive. Change, however, weaves – it coils what has happened into what will be. For me, change is a communion with what Yuwaalaraay call 'baayangali' (bye-ang-nully) or 'the natural way of things'. It harnesses people and relationships and histories and places, and invites us to build into rather than leave behind. This is what I believe Dilboong was encouraging me towards as I wrote.

The places I went to – Gadigal, Cammeraygal, Wangal – have shaped me both before and during the writing of *the belburd*. As has the Bidjigal Country the majority of the book was written on. They are all places of saltwater and sand. I honour them without acquisition. And uphold their owners' sovereignty. I am especially grateful to the baby who stretched out her arms and invited a freshwater Murri woman-writer to play.

As a First Nations woman living on and thriving in Dilboong's Country, I am a direct beneficiary of her and her family's lived experience. I therefore have an obligation not only to celebrate but credit her role in the shaping and changing of my life. I did not seek to carve my story from hers. Or to sever its belonging to her own kin. Dilboong's right story will be written by her Countrypeople in the time of their choosing. Till then, this story aims to hold that space open, cleared and ready. So many have given so that I may receive. Baby Dilboong, a glorious Blak universe, is one of many.

Thank Yous

Vanessa Radnidge, Emily Lighezzolo and Hachette Australia; Jasmin McGaughey; Rebecca Hamilton; Byron Writers Festival Indigenous Retreat; Stella Prize Writing Retreat; Peter and Kinchem Hedges at Springfield; Dr Delia Falconer, Dr Eleanor Limprecht and UTS Creative Writing Faculty; NSW Copyright Agency; Grace Heifetz and Left Bank Literary; Fabiola; The Old Ones and Yet To Come Ones; and finally, those two wadjins on the train that made me question who the universe really is.

Book Club Questions

1. *the belburd* brings together a contemporary narrative and a lyrical, almost magical fable in the one novel. How did you interpret the relationship between Ginny and Sprite, and their stories?

2. Ginny's story unfurls slowly over the course of many chapters. At first, what did you imagine she was doing with the shredder, the water and the seeds?

3. Which is your favourite Ginny Dilboong poem and why?

4. What thoughts on motherhood did Mother Eel and the birth spirits prompt in you?

5. The passage of time within Sprite's chapters is beautifully rendered. How did you feel when you realised Sprite's longing to be born wasn't matched by the length of her human life?

6. There is some powerful commentary in the book about hidden (and not-so-hidden) racism. How did this make you think about the treatment of First Nations people, both in the past and today?

7. What did you take away from *the belburd*'s final chapter? What is next for Ginny, in terms of her poetry, Dreamtime Books, and her relationships with herself and Nathan?

8. After reading this novel, what do you think about time, connection, the generations that have come before you and the cycle of life?

9. Nardi Simpson is a Yuwaalaraay woman and has described how the Yuwaalaraay people continually read Country, seasons, tracks, winds, relationships, the stars, trade routes and fires. This reading is not done with eyes alone, but engages the entirety of their bodies and spirit. How does this reflect on the way we should read *the belburd*?

Nardi Simpson is a Yuwaalaraay storyteller from New South Wales' northwest freshwater plains. As a member of Indigenous duo Stiff Gins, Nardi has travelled nationally and internationally for the past twenty-two years. She is also a founding member of Freshwater, an all-female vocal ensemble formed to revive the language and singing traditions of NSW river communities.

Nardi is a graduate of Ngarra-Burria First Peoples Composers and is currently undertaking a PhD through the Australian National University's School of Music in Composition. Nardi is the current musical director of Barayagal, a cross-cultural choir based at the Sydney Conservatorium of Music. In 2021, Nardi was First Nations artist in residence at the Sydney Conservatorium and with Ensemble Offspring.

Nardi's debut novel, *Song of the Crocodile*, won the 2017 Black&Write! Fellowship and the ALS Gold Medal, and was longlisted for the 2021 Stella Prize and Miles Franklin Literary Award. Nardi currently lives in Sydney and continues to be heavily involved in the teaching and sharing of culture in both her Sydney and Yuwaalaraay communities.